Starting with non-fiction, **Dianne Drake** penned hundreds of articles and seven books under the name JJ Despain. In 2001 she began her romance-writing career with *The Doctor Dilemma*. In 2005 Dianne's first Medical Romance, *Nurse in Recovery*, was published, and with more than twenty novels to her credit she has enjoyed writing ever since.

Also by Dianne Drake

Tortured by Her Touch
Doctor, Mummy...Wife?
The Nurse and the Single Dad
Saved by Doctor Dreamy
Bachelor Doc, Unexpected Dad

Sinclair Hospital Surgeons miniseries

Reunited with Her Army Doc
Healing Her Boss's Heart

Discover more at millsandboon.co.uk.

SECOND CHANCE WITH HER ARMY DOC

DIANNE DRAKE

MILLS & BOON

Published in Great Britain 2018
by Mills & Boon, an imprint of HarperCollins*Publishers*
1 London Bridge Street, London, SE1 9GF

ISBN: 978-0-263-07709-4

FSC
www.fsc.org
MIX
Paper from
responsible sources
FSC® C007454

This book is produced from independently certified FSC™ paper
to ensure responsible forest management.
For more information visit www.harpercollins.co.uk/green.

Printed and bound in Great Britain
by CPI Group (UK) Ltd, Croydon, CR0 4YY

To soldiers all around the world who came home
only to find the greater battle was still ahead of them.
And to Bill, who lost the battle.

PROLOGUE

THE SAND BETWEEN her toes tickled, and the moon was so bright it was as if someone had hung it on the beach just for them.

Carter always had these romantic ideas—seeing the vineyards of Napa Valley from a hot air balloon; a resort spa weekend when they'd have grapeseed massages and sip champagne in a hot mineral spring tub on their private patio, separating their world from everything else; joining in a celebration of light with a Chinese lantern inscribed with their names, sent into the nighttime sky along with hundreds of others.

And tonight, dancing on the beach in the moonlight. Feeling the gentle lapping of the water on their ankles as the tide trickled in. Seeing the far-off harbor lights twinkle against the black sky. Listening to the night birds searching for their evening meal.

"Are you chilly?" Carter asked.

"No, I'm fine," Sloane replied, snuggling even closer into his arms.

She was always fine when he held her like this. In his arms—that was where she was meant to be.

"Maybe we should leave?"

Maybe they should, but she didn't want to. Not yet.

These opportunities with Carter were scarce, due to

conflicting work schedules, and she wanted every scrap of every minute right where she was, before they had to go back.

"Or, maybe we should stay," she countered, her body rocking so sensuously against his she knew that even when they got to their room the night would be far from over. "Just for another few minutes."

Carter chuckled as he pushed the wild copper hair from her face, then bent to kiss her on the neck. "Are you sure?" he whispered, just above a kiss.

The goosebumps started immediately. They always did with Carter. And she shivered...

"See... I knew you were chilly." He gave her another kiss in the same spot, leaving a trail of butterfly kisses along her neck, ending at her jaw. "But I know where it's warm..."

In his arms. Anywhere. Anytime.

"Maybe we should go back," she whispered, a little sad that their dance had ended.

She loved Carter's spontaneity—loved the way he would simply push everything aside just to spend what little time they could together.

Last weekend a climb in the canyons. Before that scuba diving. Restaurants. Vineyards and wine-tasting. Bicycling at dusk on a coastal boardwalk, then stopping for coffee and watching the sunset.

Their moments together were so few, and yet when they did find those moments nobody else in the world existed. It was just the two of them, making the most of what they had.

"It's warm right here in your arms," said Sloane, her voice breathy with desire. She didn't want to change a moment of this, but she also didn't want to change a mo-

ment of what Carter had planned for the evening. "So one more dance, please?"

"One more," he said, then bent to her ear. "Then it's my turn to dance my way."

More goosebumps. Another shiver.

"Maybe we should save the dance on the beach for another time and go see what your dance is about."

"You know what my dance is about," he said as he scooped her up into his arms. "It's the dance that's as old as time."

She loved it when he carried her. While she wasn't particularly large, he was all muscle. Built ruggedly. Built just to fit her.

"Will there be wine?" she asked.

"If that's what you want."

There would also be white rose petals and candles, and strawberries dipped in chocolate. The reason she knew this was that she'd peeked at the bill. She hadn't meant to, but he'd left it on the dresser when he'd gone out for ice, and she hadn't been able to help herself.

Carter was always full of so many surprises—all of them for her, even if she did cheat a little in her excitement to find out. But he always made her feel like Christmas—the anticipation, the build-up of excitement, the dreaming of what he would do next.

Yes, even on the few instances she'd taken a peek, like she just had, and like she'd done when she was a little girl. Only then her dad had hidden packages of dolls and games and princess crowns, where Carter hid the little romantic things that caused her heart to beat faster—coupon books redeemable any time for kisses, hugs, making love...poems he'd written—not always good but definitely from his heart—and selfies of the two of them he'd had blown up and framed. There were at least three dozen of them on the hall wall leading to their bedroom.

But tonight there would be no selfies for what he had in store. Or maybe just one, with the two of them cuddled in the sheets. Yes, that would be nice—if she remembered. Because Carter had a way of making her forget everything but the moment.

"Are you going to be a brute and kick the door in?" she asked as they approached their room, she still in his arms.

"Oh, I'm going to be a brute—but it has nothing to do with the door."

Of course he wasn't going to be a brute. He was gentle in every way a man could be gentle, and as he lowered her to the bed and she held out her arms to him...

Sloane gasped, and bolted up in bed. Tears were streaming down her cheeks. She was actually crying in her sleep for him. For them. And tonight had been no different from when she'd had the same dream before. Night after night of it, then week after week, in one version or another.

Sometimes they'd make it to their room; sometimes they'd never even get off the beach. But there was never an ending—just the way she and Carter hadn't had a real ending.

Six years together and all she had left of him was a small jar of shrapnel from his injuries.

Dr. Sloane Manning swiped back angry tears, painful tears, then reached for her phone and punched in a number. "Yes," she said, when the party on the other end answered. "I'd like to make a reservation for one."

One. She almost choked on the word. She was going alone to a place she and Carter had always planned to explore together when they had the time. Well, *she* had the time, and most of that time was about to be invested in moving on.

“I’ll be in sometime tomorrow. Best room you’ve got, please.” Next came her credit card number, then she was set. Maybe a good hike in the desert and some nice, hard rock-climbing would snap her out of her funk.

Or maybe it wouldn’t. In any case, she was going once she’d cleared her schedule with her dad, who would make sure she was covered for the next few days. Or weeks. Either one. Because right now the last thing on her mind was surgery—which wasn’t the best situation for her patients. They deserved all of her, and she wasn’t even sure that if she was put back together she’d all be all there. So maybe going out and trying to find some of those missing pieces of herself was exactly what she needed. Because she couldn’t go on like this: not with the dreams, the tears, the broken heart…

CHAPTER ONE

"SO, AFTER YOU left Sloane, then what?" Matt McClain asked his old Army buddy Carter Holmes.

Carter cringed at the memory of how he'd left her. With a text.

Sorry, I can't do this any longer. I've got to go find myself on my own.

Sloane Manning had done everything in her power to help him. She'd come to Germany for his surgeries and stayed at his bedside for days, until he was well enough to be shipped home. Then, at home, she'd put aside practically every aspect of her own life just to help him through.

She'd found different treatment options for PTSD, and she'd stood by him when her father had hired him back at Manning Hospital, even though he clearly hadn't been ready for the stress. And she'd stood by him again when her father had suspended him for any number of the little infractions he'd incurred in his first six months back.

He'd done nothing to jeopardize a patient. Quite the opposite. He'd done everything to jeopardize his career. Insubordination. Tardiness. Bad attitude all along.

"I found a program that seemed like it might work for

me. Sloane's idea was something more traditional—like seeing a counselor or group therapy. But, that's not me. So, I looked for something else."

"And...?" Matt asked.

"I completed the first part. Did pretty well, all things considered. And my counselor there said there was excellent hope for my future. So now they've put me on a waiting list for the next part of the program, and with any luck I'll be called within the next couple of months. They give you a little time off between parts one and two, to make sure part one has taken. So...that's why I'm here, asking for a job. I need to keep myself busy until I go back to Tennessee. I need to keep my mind on the things I can control, and not on the things I can't."

"Sounds like it's working," Matt said.

"It is. It's a slow process, but little by little it's helping me define who I am again."

He and Matt had been trapped in a cave in Afghanistan when, for whatever reason, he'd snapped. Left the cave and run head-first into gunfire. He'd got hit pretty hard. Lost a kidney and a spleen as a result. Damaged his other kidney as well. Matt had risked his life to leave the relative safety of that cave to save him.

"It's a bear rescue facility. I'll work with bear cubs—rescue them if they're abandoned or injured, take care of them and, if they're able to return to the wild, get them prepared to do that. That's the hands-on part of the program. The first part was doing pretty much the same thing for myself—retraining for life in the world again. Making sure I have what it will take to work with the bears later on. It's an amazing program. Gives you a different kind of responsibility and helps you find yourself *inside* that responsibility."

Matt whistled. "Bears... I would have never guessed."

"Just the little black bear variety. Not ready to tackle the grizzlies yet." Carter chuckled. "And I'm the one who never even had a dog."

"Well, it seems to be agreeing with you."

"I hope it is," Carter said in all seriousness. "I can't live my life never knowing when something's going to trigger me. It's hell. It's also why I had to leave Sloane. She was always there, ready to help me. Maybe too much. Plus, I was breaking her heart."

Carter looked over Matt's shoulder, out the roadhouse window to the vast expanse of desert beyond them. So big, so empty. So—lonely. That was how *he'd* felt most of the time. Especially in the early days. Now, while he still wasn't better, he could see clearly enough to make distinctions about the reality of his situation. It wasn't great, but with another year or so in therapy it would improve. That was what he was aiming for, anyway.

"Anyway, I'm hoping that you can give me something to do for a while."

They were sitting in a corner booth at the Forgeburn Roadhouse, Matt drinking a beer, Carter drinking fizzy water. Booze had become a real problem in the last year. So had drugs. And while that was part of his past now, since falling off the wagon meant getting kicked out of the program, there'd been a few times he'd come close. But so far he hadn't indulged in those things since he'd left Sloane.

What was the point? Getting drunk only drove him deeper into depression. And getting high, while it may have caused him to forget momentarily, always sent him crashing back to reality, usually feeling worse than he'd felt before. It was a horrible feeling, always knowing how close to the edge he was and afraid of what might push him over.

"I don't come with a lot of guarantees these days, but I'm still a damned good doctor. That's probably the only thing I can count on."

"It's what I'm counting on too, Carter."

"Anyway, if you still think I'm worth taking a chance on, I'm yours until I get the call from The Recovery Project. And, like I mentioned when I called you last week, if I graduate from the program and you want me back, I'll be here."

No, it wasn't general surgery. But he wasn't up to that yet. Too many things to go wrong. Too many lives depending on his wavy blade. But being a good old country doctor would keep him in the profession and, hopefully, keep him out of trouble.

"Do you really think you can make the transition from being a surgeon to being a GP?"

"There are a lot of things in my life I have to change—including my attitude. And while in the long term I don't know how well I'll adjust to life outside the OR, in the short term I know I can't go back to that right now. Maybe never again. I don't know yet."

"You've come a long way," Matt said, tilting his mug back for the last sip of beer. "Last time I saw you, you were yelling at Sloane because you couldn't find your boots. It was pretty intense."

"She took a lot of abuse from me."

That was something he couldn't forgive in himself. He'd loved that woman more than life itself, but because she'd always been there she'd become the target for all his pent-up emotions. The anger would build up in him, and Sloane would be the one who took the impact of it.

"And it kept on getting worse."

"Any chance you two could get back together?"

Carter shook his head. "PTSD is a life sentence. I may

learn how to cope with it, even divert it, but there's never going to be a time when it's not waiting just below the surface. I can't take the risk of hurting her more than I already have."

"But you feel confident you can take on the part of my practice we've discussed? Because I can't keep an eye on you all the time. Like I told you before, my practice is growing, and I have a family to take care of. You're like a brother to me, but I can't look over your shoulder every minute of every day. So I need to feel good about turning you loose on the tourists, because that whole part of my practice can be a problem. You won't be treating permanent patients but rather patients who are here for only a few days. You won't have medical histories on them, and you might run into pre-existing conditions that they haven't divulged to you. There'll be all kinds of obstacles in taking on the tourist segment of my practice, and everything's going to be up to you. I'll be around if you need me, but for the most part you'll be on your own. Can you manage that?"

Doctor to the tourists in the many resorts near Forgeburn, Utah. He'd never been a GP, so it was going to be a challenge. But since he never backed down from a challenge this would probably work for him. He hoped so. Because he was ready to turn his life around. This living from moment to moment was killing him.

"My counselors think I can, or they wouldn't have sent that recommendation to you."

"But what do *you* think, Carter?"

"That I'm going to try my damnedest. Like I've told you already, I can't predict anything—can't even make any solid promises. But I want this to work, Matt. For you, because I owe you my life. And for me, because I want some kind of life back. A lot of people with PTSD don't get the opportunity you're giving me, and I don't want to mess that up."

"And what about Sloane? I know you two aren't together now, but have you talked to her about any of this?"

"No. The less involvement she has with me, the better it is for her."

That was the half-truth he always used to convince himself he'd done the right thing in leaving her. She'd taken care of him in the early days. Or tried, when he'd let her. She'd been patient and kind. But he'd given up. Backed away. He hadn't left her any choice other than to accept what he'd done—which was to leave.

"After she waited all those years for you, you're not going to try and get her back? Because, next to my Ellie, Sloane is probably the best woman I've ever known. I can't believe you can simply walk away from her the way you did and never look back."

"Oh, I look back—but all I can see are regrets. Mine. Hers. I can't go back, Matt. She deserves better than that. Better than me."

"And she's told you that?"

No, she had not. But it was what he'd known almost from his first day home.

"I was beating her down. You could see it in her. Day by day, piece by piece, I was taking everything she had away from her. I mean, she's a brilliant heart surgeon, and such a good person, but I was sucking the life out of her and I *hated* that. But for Sloane it was like the poet Poe said in his *Annabelle Lee*: 'And this maiden she lived with no other thought than to love and be loved by me.' That's all she wanted, Matt. To love me and have me love her back. But it wasn't in me anymore."

"Sorry to hear that."

"Me too—in more ways than I probably even know."

And in so many ways that he *did* know. Ways that kept him awake at night. Ways that reduced him to tears when his thoughts wouldn't be shut off.

"So, like I said, she's better off without me."

"And you? Are you better off without *her*?"

"It doesn't matter, as long as she's not part of my life anymore."

"What *is* your life, Carter? Other than the job I'm giving you here, what is your life?"

"Damned if I know. But when I figure it out, you'll be the first to know."

"That bad?" Matt asked.

"That bad," he said in earnest. "Hopefully getting better, though."

"Because of your bear rescue program?"

Carter smiled. "Because of what I hope I can do to make my little part of the program successful."

"Well, that's the attitude I'm looking for." Matt extended his hand across the table to Carter. "So, welcome to Forgeburn's only medical practice."

Carter took Matt's hand, wondering if this was too much, too soon. He was still on a high from the success he'd seen in the first part of his recovery program, but would that be enough to the job that needed to be done here?

For a while he'd ridden the crest of the self-confidence wave, but now he was underneath it. That was PTSD, though, wasn't it? Always trying to rob you of yourself. Always chipping away at the bits and pieces that seemed to be moving forward.

There was a time when his normal reaction would have been to say, *I've got this*. Now, though, he wasn't sure what he had—and that was what scared him. Before PTSD, nothing ever had. Now, almost everything did.

But this was the opportunity he needed. So it was time to put one foot forward and hope he could stay there for a while.

"When do you want me to start?"

Sloane Manning looked at the text messages on her phone, then at her phone messages. Still nothing. She'd been trying to call Carter for weeks. At least once a day. Sometimes twice. Not that there was much to say at this point. But she was concerned. Six years of her life had gone into that man—most of it waiting while he was in the military—and it wasn't easy to detach herself from the life she'd expected to have by now.

After her father had dismissed Carter from his job at the hospital he'd disappeared. Hadn't packed anything to speak of. Hadn't said goodbye or even left a note other than a vague text message. The only thing that had told her Carter was gone was that their apartment—*her* apartment—seemed so hollow and cold now. She hated being there. Hated being by herself there. Because it was *their* home, not hers.

Which was why she was moving back in with her dad when she got back from this two-week vacation. She'd waited long enough for Carter to make a move. But after three months it was clear he wasn't going to do that. In fact she didn't even know where he was. He'd been in Vegas for a while, but after that…

So here she was at the airport, ready to board a plane to one of the places she and Carter had always talked about. She was ready to give herself some good, hard physical licks in the canyons and the desert. Ready to start over on her own.

"Dr. Sloane Manning," the attendant at the desk called over the loudspeaker. "Last call for Dr. Sloane Manning."

Hearing her name startled her out of her thoughts, and almost in a panic she grabbed up her carry-on bag and ran toward the check-in before the loading gate shut.

"Sorry about that," she said to the attendant. "I was…"

What? Daydreaming about a romance gone bad? Everybody had one, didn't they? So why would the gate attendant care about hers?

"I was preoccupied."

The gate attendant made it clear that she didn't care, and that all she wanted was to get Sloane on the plane and start focusing on the next group of passengers, already filing in to catch the next flight.

So, Sloane hustled herself through, took her seat in the third row of the first-class section, leaned her head back against the headrest and hoped people would assume her to be asleep and leave her alone. The way Carter had done the last few months of their relationship. She in one bedroom, he in the other. Barely talking when they met in the hall. Barely even acknowledging each other's existence unless it was absolutely necessary.

With her eyes shut she could visualize everything. The apathy. The temper. The outrage. But most of all the pain. She could still feel it burrowing in, winding its corkscrew tentacles around every fiber of her being.

"Still no luck?" Gemma Hastings, Sloane's surgical assistant, had asked, when she'd informed her people early that morning that she'd be gone for a couple of weeks.

"It's done," she'd told her. "I've hung on too long and too hard. It's time to get myself sorted and start moving in a new direction."

What that direction was, she didn't know. But if she didn't move in some other direction soon, she was afraid she might never move at all. Her friends, even her dad, had been telling her this was what she needed to do. So, after three months she was finally taking their advice. She was taking some *me time* to readjust.

As for loving Carter—tossing that away wouldn't be as easy as stepping onto a plane and hiding out for a while. Still, what was the point in worrying about him when he didn't worry about himself? Or worry about them?

That was the worst of it. He'd given up on *them*. And quite easily. But here she was, still hanging on. Why? Maybe her feelings for Carter were some sort of remnant, left over from the days when she'd first fallen in love with him, when he had been kind and good, and the best surgeon she'd ever seen. Maybe her love was nothing more than an old habit she didn't know how to break.

Because she still loved him?

That was the question she didn't want to answer, because the answer might scare her. Falling in love with one man, then watching him turn into someone else she didn't even recognize had been tough. Trying to stay in love with the man he'd turned into had been even tougher, because there had still been parts of the Carter she'd known left and she'd been able to see them struggling to get out.

But she'd also been able to see Carter struggling to keep them locked away.

She thought about the day they'd met. She'd already heard about him from her father.

"He's supposed to be the best of the best," Harlan Manning had said. "Good at everything he does and full of adventure—which he says keeps him from getting dull."

"Will he fit in here?" she'd asked her dad. "We're a conservative little surgery in most regards. Everybody knows everybody else. There's never any in-fighting, the way I saw it going on during my residency in Boston."

Generally everybody got along, did their jobs, and walked away contented. But from the description of Carter Holmes she'd had some qualms, because he'd seemed so—*out there*. He liked big sports—skydiving, mountain-climbing, motorcycling. And he liked the ladies.

That was only his personal reputation—which she totally forgot when she first laid eyes on him. Carter was tall, muscular. Deep, penetrating gray eyes. Dark brown hair, short-cut in a messy, sticking-out style which looked *so* good on him. Three days' growth of dark stubble which had made her go weak in the knees, imagining what it would feel like on her skin. And that smile of his…

OMG, it could knock a girl off her feet, it was so sexy.

He'd put all that masculinity to good use, too, asking the hospital owner's daughter out after only knowing her for five minutes.

Of course she'd said yes. What else could she have done? She'd been smitten at first sight, sexually attracted at second, and in love at third. Well, maybe not real love. But that had come about pretty quickly when, after their first evening together, Carter never went home. Not the next day either, or the day after that. In fact by the third day he had totally moved in to her tiny apartment, making himself right at home as if he'd always been there.

"For what it's worth, Sloane, Carter was crazy about you," her assistant had said. "Everybody could see that. So maybe if he gets himself straightened out…"

"*If,*" she'd responded. "Not going to hold my breath on that one."

But she was. Every minute of every hour of every

day. And it was causing her to be distracted in her operating room. Distraction and heart surgery didn't mix, and if it continued, she'd either have to step down from her position voluntarily, or her father—in his position as chief—would remove her. He didn't play favorites when it came to patient care, and she was included in that. So, her distraction could conceivably cost her her job. Which was why she had to get away to sort it out. And maybe Forgeburn, Utah, wasn't the hub of the universe, but it *was* beautiful, according to Matt McClain, an old friend.

She'd met him through Carter, and liked him right off. He lived in Forgeburn now, so why not visit? Maybe Matt would have a different insight into Carter than she did.

So, her goal was to sort it out, get over it, then get back to a life where she was in control of herself again—her life as it had been before Carter's PTSD. She'd had goals then: becoming the head of cardiac surgery at Manning, having a family, a beautiful life. Then PTSD had happened and everything had changed.

"Thank you, Carter Holmes," she whispered as the pilot announced it was time to prepare for landing. "Thank you for nothing."

Matt's clinic was a few miles away. He'd made that perfectly clear. Which was fine, because it was time for Carter to see if his own two feet would hold him up again.

For that he needed space—and Forgeburn, Utah, had plenty of that. He also needed to be successful here, because getting back to his recovery program was contingent upon that. If he succeeded here, he moved forward in the program. If he failed, he moved back to square one and started all over. If he was lucky.

Being kicked out of the program was a setback Carter didn't want. What was more, if he got sent back to the beginning, did he have enough left in him to fight his way through it again? He didn't trust himself enough to believe he could.

Of course he did have a job in medicine again, a place to stay, and a small salary. Life wasn't great, but it was better, and apologizing to his best buddy was the first step in what he hoped would be many more steps in the right direction.

But not in Sloane's direction. That much he was sure of.

"This will be fine," he said to Dexter Doyle, the owner of what had to be the worst hotel within a hundred miles.

So here he was in his new home—one room with a double bed, a toilet, mini-fridge, microwave, desk and chair—all of it dated. It wasn't the best place he'd ever stayed, but not the worst either. Maybe it was more like a reflection of his life. All the right equipment, but all of it dated—almost to the point of no recognition. Well, *he* was the one who'd walked out on the best living situation he'd ever had, so he couldn't really complain.

"Is there a liquor store around here?" he asked, tossing his duffle bag on the bed, hoping bed bugs wouldn't scurry out.

"A couple miles up the road."

"And a television?" Carter asked, noticing the room didn't have one.

"Out for repair."

"I don't suppose you offer a wake-up call?"

He remembered the way Sloane had used to wake him up. Always with a smile, and a kiss, and a cup of coffee. Often a whole lot more. Her touch. Her red hair brushing across his face. The mintiness of her breath when she kissed him. Yes, those were the mornings he'd loved waking up.

Dexter pointed to the old digital clock next to the bed. "If you want to wake up, set the alarm."

"Well, then…" Carter said, sitting down on the bed to test it. As he'd suspected, lumpy and saggy. "Looks like I'm home." For a while, anyway."

But he was anxious to return to Tennessee, so he could work toward the next part of his life—whatever that turned out to be.

Upwards and onwards, he thought as he settled into his room. Things were looking up. Especially now that he wasn't around Sloane any longer. So, on the one hand he liked the feeling of freedom and the optimism that went with it. But on the other he missed his life with Sloane.

It was an ache that had left a hole that would never be filled. But for Sloane he had to endure it and follow the course. More than that, he had to get used to the ache—because she couldn't be part of him anymore. Not in a real sense. In an emotional sense. However, he'd never let her go. Not now. Not ever. Falling in love with her the way he had didn't leave room for anything or anyone else. Meaning his destiny was set. And it was going to be a lonely one.

For Sloane, though…he'd do anything.

Next morning, when Carter surveyed his new office, he was neither pleased nor displeased with it; he was mainly ambivalent. That was the way so many of his days seemed to go, unless he made a hard effort to fight through it.

This morning he hadn't started his fight yet. It would happen, though. Once he got himself involved he'd find his way through, instead of dwelling somewhere in the middle of it like he'd used to do.

He took another look at it his office. It was basic, but

well-equipped. Spotlessly clean, with fresh paint. The white on every wall put him off a little, but color really didn't matter when the basic medical tools were at his disposal.

The truth was, it wasn't a bad little office, all things considered. Two exam rooms, a spacious storage closet, a reception area and an office. Matt would subsidize his rent at the hotel and the office for now, and then if Tennessee worked out for him, and he was good enough to come back here full time, he would take over the costs himself and buy out this part of Matt's practice.

If things didn't work that way… Well, he didn't know what came after that. As he'd been told, over and over, by his recovery counselor, *"Take it one day at a time, and strive to make that day the best day ever."*

In other words, he was not to mess up his mind with the future when getting through the current day was never guaranteed. It made sense—especially since he was given to projecting his future and that, so often, turned into a PTSD trigger.

Whenever it took him over he could almost feel the impending flare-up course through his veins. His vision blurred, his hands shook, his head felt as if it was ready to explode. He was like a fire-breathing dragon, puffing up and getting ready for his next battle.

Unfortunately Carter's "next battle" had cost him dearly. His job, the love of his life… And now he was in Forgeburn, running a storefront clinic for seasonal tourists, and a handful of locals who lived closer to Carter's part of the practice than Matt's, keeping his fingers crossed that he'd survive this day and make it through till tomorrow.

On the door peg, in the room marked *Office*, hung

a crisp new lab jacket. Carter smiled—maybe the first smile that had cracked his face in weeks or months.

At least he hadn't lost his license to practice. That was good, despite the fact he'd lost everything else. He liked being a doctor. No, he *loved* being a doctor. It was all he'd ever wanted from the time he'd been a kid.

When all his friends had been vacillating between fireman, policeman and whatever else all little boys wanted to be at some point in their lives, being a doctor had been it for him, because he had wanted to find a way to cure his brother James. Carter had promised James he would, when he was nine and James had been on his last days, dying from cystic fibrosis.

Two years younger than Carter, James had spent his whole life in and out of hospitals. He'd never been strong enough to walk more than a few steps, and he'd never breathed well enough to go outside and play—not even for a few minutes. For James, life had been all tests and procedures, and somewhere in Carter's nine-year-old mind he'd thought if he made a promise to save his brother and make him well it would happen. And it would give his entire family some hope to cling to.

But a week after his promise his dad had been sitting on the front step crying when Carter had arrived home from school. And after that, unlike his friends, who had gone back and forth on what they wanted to be, he never had. He'd been angry at the world for taking his brother. Angry at himself that he hadn't been able to do more. Angry at the doctors who'd always predicted a grave outcome for his brother.

He'd expected them to do better. Expected them to produce a miracle. Expected them to offer hope rather than rip it away. Which was why he'd become a doctor—a surgeon. Because he wanted to do the things that hadn't been done for his brother. Of course, the closer Carter had come to his goal, the more he'd realized that some outcomes would break his heart no matter what he did. That was part of the profession. But that hadn't discouraged him, because many more outcomes were good. And it was those outcomes he always dedicated to his brother—without fail.

But now—well, now he was a GP. And he was grateful for that. Maybe it was the only thing left in his life he had to be grateful for, since he'd destroyed everything else that mattered.

"It's nice," Carter said to the twenty-something girl who'd been following him from room to room: Marcie, his new receptionist.

Her father owned the building and had seized the opportunity to lower the rent if the medical practice employed her. Apparently, Marcie had never worked a day in her life and this was to be her first ever job. Matt had hired her since, legally, this was *his* practice.

"Daddy had it painted fresh," she said, her nose in her phone, scrolling, scrolling… Short skirt, long vest, tall boots, pinkish yellow hair… Not the professional image he'd hoped for. But a discount was a discount, and he'd have to make the best of his workforce virgin.

He actually chuckled. If his life weren't so pathetic this could be funny. It wasn't, though. Nobody could screw up so many things the way he had and call it funny. But, like he'd told Matt, he was a good doctor. That was the only sure thing he had to hang on to—his medical skills. Maybe—somehow—he wouldn't mess those up, too.

"So, how about we open up for business tomorrow morning?" he asked Marcie.

Her reply was a head nod as she continued to scroll.

Who was it that had said something about fastening

up for a bumpy ride? Well, this was *his* bumpy ride, but he wasn't sure he was fastened up enough for it.

Time would tell, he supposed.

CHAPTER TWO

SO THIS WAS FORGEBURN. Sloane looked up and down the main drag, not sure whether she liked it or not. For sure, it was remote. And small. So small, in fact, that she could see both ends of town from her vantage point at the gas station in the middle.

It did have some appeal, she decided, as her gaze came to rest on a good-looking foothill that seemed as if it needed an experienced climber on it. It was red clay, not too steep, but steep enough that she knew her climbing skills—the skills Carter had taught her—would get her to the top. Something she would definitely do, since she was booked here in Forgeburn for the entire two weeks of her vacation.

Hiking the desert, climbing the rocks, dropping down into some of the canyons—these were all things she'd never done Before Carter, as she called it now. But they were things she loved doing now, along with scuba diving, parasailing, mountain biking, and so many other outdoor recreational activities.

She missed all those—missed doing them with Carter. Missed the way he'd congratulate her when she achieved something she'd never done before. First the congratulatory hug, then the congratulatory kiss, then the congratulatory run to the bedroom for the best congratulatory practice of all.

Yes, she missed all that. Missed the emotion and the elation. Missed the physical contact, even if it was a hug of condolence when she didn't achieve what she'd set out to do.

So… Forgeburn—she could see why Carter had talked about it so much. They'd planned on a visit—something longer than the two or three days off they usually got. And here she was, with all the time in the world. But alone.

She could have gone someplace else. Anyplace else. And maybe she should have. But here, with so much to remind her of what she no longer had, maybe she would start to remind herself that she no longer had Carter either.

Sighing, Sloane finished pumping gas into her car, then took one more look around before she headed down the road to Red Rock Canyon Resort—her home away from home for the next two weeks. Right now she felt—*nothing.* Carter had told her he'd felt that way much of the time and now she finally understood it herself. It was so empty. So lonely.

Good move coming here? Or bad move?

Either way, she was here, and there was plenty to do—or nothing, if that was what she chose. Her real choice, however, wouldn't happen, because that involved sleeping out under the stars somewhere, listening to the coyotes howl. Curling up with Carter in a single sleeping bag. Making love under the stars. And this evening promised a sky full of beautiful stars.

"Could you tell me if there are any evening hikes in the desert?" she asked the concierge as she checked in to the Red Rock Canyon Resort.

"We have one leaving in about an hour. It's five miles, and it leads into the desert to explore various constellations that are visible only because there's no city lighting getting in the way. But you must have your own hiking gear, as our rental facility is closed."

"Sounds perfect to me. If there's space, sign me up."

"We have other less strenuous options in the morning," said the concierge, Diego Sanchez. "Perhaps you'd rather wait, *señorita*?"

"No. I'd rather go tonight. And strenuous is good. Just what I need."

"Then I'll pass your name along to our tour guide. He'll contact you shortly about the equipment you need to bring. You *do* have equipment, don't you?"

Everything that Carter had ever bought her. She'd thought about throwing it all away and starting over, but for now it was all she had, and she hoped she would be able to use it without too many memories hiking along with her.

Even so, as she went to her room to get ready, memories were already creeping in—like how his temper had flared for no reason. When he'd panicked at an unexpected loud noise. And then there had been the nightmares, the flashbacks and triggers. And finally, a slow-growing lack of trust in *her*.

Before he'd gone into the Army he'd trusted her implicitly. When he'd come home he'd seemed wary of her at first. Then eventually mistrusting. That had maybe been the worst of everything. Planning a life with someone who didn't trust her. That was when she'd started to wonder if she should, or could, go through with their marriage. Or simply put it on hold for a while.

After all, she'd already invested six years—what was another year or so on top of that?

Carter had answered that question by leaving before she'd had a chance to decide.

Up and down. That had been her life with Carter after he'd come home. That and her concern for his health, since he'd refused to see a nephrologist about his kidney condition. He'd needed to keep the remaining kidney healthy, but everything he'd done had seemed to contradict that.

Still, she'd stayed with him even when it had become clear that their feelings for each other were eroding, because she'd known who was underneath all that trauma—known the man he really was even though he hadn't anymore. And because she'd loved him, and some of that love had still been hanging on for dear life.

In the end, though, love hadn't been enough. And now here she was in Forgeburn, getting ready to look at the stars, hoping to find the one thing that would turn her in the direction that led her away from Carter once and for all. Because she sure wasn't headed toward him now.

After lacing up her hiking boots, then tucking a few necessary supplies into the pockets of her cargo vest, Sloane looked at herself in the mirror. No wrinkles yet, which surprised her, with the way she worried. But there were bags under her eyes. Still cosmetically fixable, but there all the same. Yes, she definitely needed this vacation, she thought as she pulled her wild copper hair into a ponytail, then put a cap on her head.

"Ready," she said to herself as she headed toward the door. But was she really? If it was rest she needed, and time to think, why was she already filling her schedule with activities.

Because if she kept herself busy she wouldn't have to think. And sometimes thinking hurt too much.

* * *

"Are you a walk-in, or do you have an appointment?" the young girl at the desk asked Sloane, without looking up. The girl was buried in her phone.

"Walk-in. All I need are a few stitches for this cut on my leg."

One of the other night hikers had knocked her into the face of a rather jagged rock in his enthusiasm to get a better look at Venus and Mars, which were less than a degree apart. He been all excited that Jupiter was also nearby.

It had been a beautiful sight, with Venus by far being the brightest of the three. Of course when she'd managed to distinguish Venus from the rest of the planets her mind had drifted off to something far less astrological. In fact she had been contemplating Venus as the Roman goddess of love, sexuality, beauty, prosperity and fertility when the night hiker had clipped her and sent her into an undignified sprawl.

Now she needed stitches and antibiotics.

She could have gone to see Matt, but he would be such a reminder that she wasn't sure she was ready to face him. He and Carter had been so close once upon a time. Like brothers. But, like everything else with Carter, that friendship had died as well.

She would look Matt up. It was inevitable that she would see him at some point in her stay here. But not now—she wasn't ready. So as soon as morning had forced her to open her eyes, she'd asked about the nearest doctor. She had been told there was a tourist doctor nearby, and where she could find his office, and now here she was, seeking medical care.

The young girl leaned over the desk to appraise the cut, then settled back down into her chair.

"I'll put you on the list and he'll see you as soon as…" She shrugged. "When he's ready."

It was a plain office. Not much to look at. No outdated magazines to read. But it was freshly painted. She could still smell the remnants of new paint.

"How long have you been here?" she asked the girl.

She looked up from her phone and said, "We're new. Just opened."

"Is the doctor Matt McClain?" she asked, hoping it was not.

"Nope. He takes care of the cowboys. We're strictly here for the tourists, who get injured doing things like whatever it was *you* were doing that got you cut up."

"Do you need my name for your records?" Sloane asked.

"Doc will take care of that."

"Will he take care of my insurance papers as well?" This was an oddly run practice and she wondered what kind of doctor allowed it.

"Well, he won't let *me* do them, so I guess it's up to him."

Definitely odd. And if she'd needed something more than stitches she'd probably have gone looking for Matt. But she was here now and, since there'd been no other cars in the parking lot, it shouldn't be too long before she got called in.

She was right. Within another couple of minutes the receptionist gave her a wave to go on back, without so much as looking up from her phone.

So she took it upon herself to wander down the hall, find the exam room, then sit up on the exam table and wait. Another minute passed before she heard footsteps heading down the hall and her blood froze in her veins.

No, it couldn't be. She knew those footsteps. Knew them by heart.

Consequently, when the doctor pushed open the door, Sloane's head started to spin. "What are you doing here?" she asked, trying to hold back on her wobbly voice.

"Sloane? What are *you* doing here?" He closed the exam room door behind him but made no attempt to walk over to her.

"I asked you first," she said.

"I'm trying to start over. Matt gave me a job here. He needed help, I needed help…so it worked out. Now you."

"Vacation. I came here because—Well, I didn't know you were here. Last I heard you were in Vegas."

"Actually, Tennessee," he said. "Vegas before that."

"Now you're *here*? Seriously?"

"As serious as it gets. So, I'm assuming you want me to stitch up that cut on your leg?"

She'd almost forgotten about that, she was so flustered. "It happened last night. I was out stargazing and met up with the sharp end of a rock."

"Since when do you stargaze?" he asked, finally walking over to the exam table.

"Since last night."

"And what did you learn?"

"That Venus shines the brightest and it's best to stargaze on your own, or with a sure-footed friend."

"Meaning…?"

"Meaning I did the tourist thing and now I'm paying for it. So, why here, Carter? I'm assuming Matt gave you an opportunity, but you're clearly not working as a surgeon. More like what? A GP?"

"Exactly," he said, as he bent to assess the cut.

"But you've never done that kind of work."

"And *you've* never gone stargazing. So, I suppose we

file it all under 'first time'." He looked up at her. "Everything has to start somewhere, doesn't it?" Then he ran his hand down the calf of her leg.

Sloane shivered to his touch the way she always had. "Why are you touching me that way?" she asked. "We're over. You quit touching me that way months ago."

He took his hand off her leg, stood up and smiled.

"Actually, that was a perfectly good GP's assessment. I wanted to make sure your leg wasn't too warm, which might indicate an infection setting in."

"I'm a doctor. I know to disinfect it."

"And I'm a doctor, too. A doctor who's trying his hardest to be a *good* doctor."

"You always were good, Carter. Nobody ever questioned that. It was everything else that went with you…"

"My attitude?"

Sloane let out a deep sigh. She hadn't come on vacation to start this whole thing over again. She was trying to get away from it. Sort it out and put it behind her. But how could she do that when Carter was here?

"I've said all there is to say about your attitude. So how about the stitches?"

"I'd prefer to butterfly it. Less chance of scarring."

Butterfly stitches were not exactly stitches, but thin strips with an adhesive backing used to close small wounds.

"Oh, and when was the last time you had a tetanus shot?"

"Good on the butterfly stitches. Much better than needle and thread. And as for the tetanus shot…"

She shrugged her shoulders. She should know, but she didn't. Like most people, she didn't keep track of those sorts of things. Although she could have told him the exact date and time of the last gamma globulin shot *he* had taken.

It had happened because of a needle stick. One of his patients—a child—had got belligerent and whacked Carter a good one as he'd been trying to give the boy a shot to calm him down before an appendectomy. Carter had already administered a mild sedative when the boy had started flailing and caught Carter's hand. The one with the used hypodermic needle still in it.

The puncture hadn't been bad, or deep, but hospital policy had demanded a visit from the old gamma globulin needle to help give Carter a temporary boost in his immune system. Which had turned out to be a good thing since, as it had happened, the kid had been in the very early stages of chickenpox.

That had been one month and thirteen days before he'd shipped out to Afghanistan. So why did she remember that when she couldn't remember her own last tetanus?

"No clue," she told him, recalling the sexy way he'd dropped his pants so she could stick him in the butt with the needle. It had been slow, seductive, and it had definitely raised her libido a notch or two. In fact, had they not been in one of the hospital exam rooms, the way his pants had slid over his hips would have definitely led to something very unprofessional. And very good.

Even thinking about it caused heat to rush to her cheeks—and for a redhead that was a disaster, because it made her look like a beet.

"You OK?" he asked as he pulled the necessary supplies from a cabinet next to the exam table.

"Just tired. Which is why I came here."

"Well, that color you're wearing right now isn't your *I'm tired* color. Normally that's more pasty and white. In fact, as I recall, that color is your—"

"Just stop it, Carter! I didn't come here to rehash old times. I need some stitches and a tetanus shot. If you can't do that, I'll go find Matt and ask him to."

"He didn't tell you I was here? Because what are the chances that you'd simply bump into me in the middle of nowhere?"

He picked up a bottle of disinfectant and squirted some on her leg.

"When I saw you sitting on my table I assumed you were here to find me."

"Trust me, Carter. You're the last person I wanted or expected to find here. And, no, Matt didn't say a word."

Which made her wonder if Matt was trying to get them back together. Surprise meeting in a desert in the middle of nowhere? Maybe it was a coincidence. Or maybe not. Right now, she didn't care. She just wanted Carter to fix her leg so she could get out of there.

Carter hadn't expected to see Sloane in Forgeburn, of all places, and now that she was here he wasn't sure what to do about it. Stay away from her altogether? Allow a small amount of cordiality in? Just what was the etiquette here? What etiquette was involved in meeting up with the woman you'd loved for so long, then dumped?

He knew Sloane in every way one person could know another, so it wasn't as if they were strangers caught up in a chance meeting. Something like that would have been easier to deal with. They could have shared general chit chat, a string of pleasantries, talked about the weather—except, Sloane deserved more than the weather forecast.

The problem was, he didn't have more. Not for her, anyway. It was too difficult, too painful, and he didn't want to go on hurting her over and over.

"The wound is clean and, as cuts go, the edges are

good. So I'm going to use about ten butterflies, then wrap it in gauze. If you're still here in a couple of days come back for a check. Or go to your own doctor when you get back home."

Which he hoped she would do—go home. Today. Right now.

"I'm here for two weeks," she said. "It's the first vacation I've had since… Well—that week you were on leave from the Army. You came home and we took a cruise down to Mexico. What was that? Four years ago?"

He knew exactly when it had been, but he didn't want memories of that week popping into his mind. It had been too nice, and they'd gotten so close. Closer than they'd been even after two years together. It was when he'd proposed to her. Well, it had been a pre-proposal—one of those *If I were to ask you, would you marry me?* sort of things.

It hadn't been until almost two years later that he'd done the real asking. And then it had been by satellite hook-up. It had been her birthday, and her friends and family had been having a party. He'd been left out, of course, being overseas. So when they'd talked later that night the question had simply popped right out of him, surprising him almost as much as it had her.

Marriage had always been his intention, though. Women like Sloane didn't come along every day, and he had been so head-over-heels crazy in love with her, almost at first sight, he hadn't been about to lose her. But he'd wanted to wait until he got home and do the proposal the right way, on a romantic weekend on the beach, or maybe up in wine country.

Somehow he'd seen it happening at dawn, not dusk. They'd be strolling hand in hand, wherever they were, and when they stopped for a break he would pull an engagement ring box from his pocket. Or they would be having brunch, sipping mimosas, and he would discreetly slide the ring box across the table.

That had been the other Carter Holmes, though. The one who'd replaced him didn't have a romantic bone in his body. Even reminding himself of the things he'd thought before made his hands shake.

"I'm going to give you a prescription for an antibiotic. There's a pharmacy about ten miles down the road. You can fill it there. If I remember correctly, you were allergic to—"

Damn, why did he have to remember so many things about her? He'd been trying not to since he'd left, and on good days he sometimes succeeded. Now, though, everything was coming back. More than he wanted. More than he could deal with.

"Penicillin," Sloane said, sliding off the exam table then bending down to straighten out her pants. "So, how much do I owe you for today?" she asked as she straightened up and looked him directly in the eye.

"Really, Sloane? Do you think I'd charge you for this?"

"To be honest, I don't know *what* you'd do. I didn't expect you to leave me without an explanation, but you did. I didn't expect you not to return my calls and texts for three months, but you did. I didn't even expect you to join the Army, but you did. So, tell me… How am I supposed to anticipate your next move, Carter? How am I supposed to know what you will and will not do?"

"I know I didn't do things the way I should have, but…"

But what? What was his excuse? He'd been doing it for her? She wouldn't believe that, even though it was the truth.

"But what's done is done, and I can't go back and change things."

"No, you can't. Neither of us can." She headed for the exam room door, then stopped and turned back to face him. "Look, us being here at the same time is a coincidence. But could we find some time when we could get together and talk? I have questions, Carter. And I deserve answers."

"Let me figure out my schedule, then I'll get back to you. Do you still have the same cell number?"

"*I'm* not the one who changed, Carter. You are. Yes, it's still the same. I didn't want to change it in case you actually did try to call or text me."

During his few hazy weeks in Vegas the last thing he had wanted to do was return her calls and have her figure out that he was even deeper into the pit than he'd been before he'd left. His drinking had been worse. He'd been taking those pills. And gambling… All the things that had distracted him from what was real.

Then in Tennessee cell phones had been confiscated and handed back only for emergencies and once-a-week contact with family or a loved one. Since he'd had no family then, or even a loved one, there'd never been any reason to ask for his cell phone back for that one allotted hour.

"I wasn't exactly in a position to reach out to anybody. It was rude, and I'm sorry, but that's who I was then."

"And not now?" she asked him before she left his office.

"It's complicated, Sloane."

And he couldn't make promises, or even lead her in the direction of thinking that he might be getting better because he didn't know if he was. Time would tell, he supposed. Time and new surroundings. But how could he tell her that? How could he tell her that *she* was part of the past he was running from?

"Life is complicated, Carter," she said. "For everybody in some way."

He sounded so—not bitter, more like apathetic. As if he'd given up or given himself over to his battle.

"So you've given up?"

"It's called hitting rock bottom." He took a couple steps toward her, then stopped, as if a barrier had been lobbed into his path. "And my choice is to not drag anybody else down with me."

"You owe me an explanation, Carter."

"For what? For losing one kidney and a spleen to shrapnel? Damaging my other kidney? For PTSD after too much gunfire, too much death, too many people to save that I couldn't? Is that what you want to hear? Because if it is I've said it all before and look where it's gotten me."

She wanted to see some emotion—some of the old Carter trying to fight back. But what she saw in his face was—*nothing*. His eyes were blank. His expression resigned.

This wasn't the Carter she'd used to know. Used to love. Not at all. This was a different man. One she didn't understand. Couldn't explain. One who seemed to be calculating every facial expression and every word. She'd been through so much with him, but this—it broke off another piece of her heart.

"You still drinking?" she asked him, not sure why she was even bothering.

He shook his head. "Gave up the pills, too. Momentary interruptions in my process are only that—momentary. Then it all comes back. So, what are you really doing here? Come to save me from myself?"

"I'm on vacation, like I told you."

But she wondered if subconsciously she'd chosen Forgeburn not so much expecting to find him here but to be closer to a part of his life when his life had been good. He and Matt had made so many plans about biking, hiking and climbing over the years, and it was something Carter had talked about so often. Getting back to his roots, he'd say, even though he wasn't from the area. Maybe the sentiment had appealed to him, or maybe it had simply been the need to step out of his problems for a while.

Whatever it was, could she have actually come here expecting to find answers? Or even expecting to find Carter himself?

"You'd talked about the area so often—maybe I thought I could find some kind of closure here. You took that from me, you know."

"I know I did," he said.

His voice was soft now. The animosity was gone, replaced by a sadness he couldn't conceal. At least not from the woman who'd loved him for so long.

"It was never my intention to hurt people—most of all you. But that's how it turned out, and in the end who cares? Who really gives a good damn?"

"I do—did," she said, fighting back tears.

She'd promised herself she wouldn't cry. That no matter what Carter said or did she wouldn't let him reduce her to that again. But here she was, fighting it because her heart was breaking yet one more time. For her—and for Carter.

"I cared."

"You should have never waited for me, Sloane. You could have had better. We both knew that."

For an instant his expression changed. Did she see regret? Or a sadness deeper than anything she'd ever seen from him before? It was there and gone so quickly she didn't know, but in that instant she'd seen Carter. The real Carter. He was still there, which did give her hope. Not for their relationship. That was over, and she had to reconcile herself to that. But she did hold out some hope for Carter—something she hadn't done in a long, long time.

"Maybe that's what you thought," she said, "but it's not what I thought."

Standing on tiptoes, she brushed a light kiss to his cheek, then backed away.

"What I knew was that I still loved you, but you didn't still love me. That's a difficult adjustment to make after so many years. I wish I could have done better at it. But I suppose that's a moot point, isn't it? Since you made the final decision about *us* without me."

Sloane didn't know whether to laugh or cry. Sitting in her rental car in the parking lot, she was too unsteady to go anywhere yet. Maybe the kiss had been a mistake—maybe it had been the last thing he wanted from her—but it had told her something she wasn't prepared to know. She still loved him. Maybe not in the breathless way she'd loved him at first, but in a more deep-down sense. It was something more profound—something she didn't understand and wasn't ready to think about.

Carter was a handsome man and, while she'd rarely let a man turn her head, she'd always reacted to him. He'd taken off some weight since she'd last seen him, and it looked good. Was he working out again? Because for the first time since he'd been injured he looked toned.

But he'd always been a head-turner, hadn't he? Sometimes he'd shown up for work in tight leather pants, which had given all the ladies quite a show before he gave himself over to his day and changed into scrubs.

She'd loved that side of him because he'd known what he was doing—had had fun with it. He'd loved having people looking at him, speculating about who he really was—a bad boy or simply a narcissist. In truth, he had been neither. Carter Holmes had simply been a man who'd enjoyed life. He'd liked to play around with it to see what turned up. And he'd taught her to enjoy it along with him. To be spontaneous. To let go occasionally and live in the moment.

That hadn't been her when they'd first met. After her mother died she'd been raised by a loving but very serious father who'd overwhelmed her with his serious world. Yet Carter had made her life so—*good.* So much fun to anticipate.

Those days were so far in the past, though, she almost wondered if they'd happened at all. Nothing seemed real anymore. It hadn't for such a long time. Even now—being here and discovering Carter was here as well—was an altered reality, and the pieces of it hadn't come together in her mind yet.

"I didn't want to stir the pot," Matt said to her an hour later, when she went to his surgery and challenged him about not telling her that Carter was in Forgeburn.

"So you just let me bump into him accidentally?" She shook her head, angry because of so many things.

"There was no guarantee you *would* bump into him."

"Yeah, right. This is *Forgeburn*, Matt. It's only a ten-minute drive from one end of the town to the other. How could I *not* bump into him?"

Matt looked out into his waiting room. Today it was overflowing with patients.

"Look, Sloane… When you called me and told me you might come here for a few days Carter and I hadn't made any specific plans yet. And, honestly, neither of you told me how bad it was between you. Carter said something to the effect that you were having problems, but I didn't know until after he was here that they were permanent problems. By then you were already on your way. So don't blame me for what you and Carter have or don't have going on. I'm only the bystander who's watching the world cave in around two of my friends."

Sloane did understand his position, but that didn't make things better. Nothing did right now, so she decided to head back to her hotel, shut herself in her room, and decide whether she should stay or go.

In so many ways she wanted to stay—maybe simply to find some closure. That was her due, and she hadn't had it—not with the way Carter had left her. But leaving wasn't such a bad idea either. This time *she'd* be the one to walk away. There would be a certain satisfaction in that.

But acting that way wasn't who Sloane was. She'd loved that man for too long, and because of everything he had been through she had no desire to hurt him. If—and that was a great big *if*—he still cared enough to be hurt.

Sloane didn't know if that was even possible. Or if what she might do would hurt *her* even more than before. It was a lot to think about. But she wasn't in the mood to think, or to do anything that related to Carter.

Except, despite her best efforts, Sloane still couldn't get him off her mind, and she was suddenly afraid that she might slip back to where she had been three months ago, when he'd left her. Not that she'd come very far from that position up until now. Still, she didn't want to backslide.

But with Carter so close to her now was there any kind of chance she could really move forward? Or even move on? She hoped so. But there was no confidence backing that hope. None whatsoever.

CHAPTER THREE

CARTER EMPTIED THE bottle of cheap whiskey he'd just bought down the drain, then placed the empty bottle on the stand next to his bed and stared at it. Cheap booze, expensive booze—it was all there, waiting for him to take that first drink. No one would know if he did. No one would care, either. But the bottle reminded him of where he was trying to go. And, that's what he still needed so much of the time. A reminder of where he'd been and how bad it was. A reminder of all the things he'd lost, that he couldn't get back. But it was also there to show him the way out if there was a way to get out.

This was *his* hell to pay, though. *His* test to achieve. To conquer. So the damned bottle would sit there and taunt him for as long as he needed to be taunted. If that was forever, so be it. But because of The Recovery Project there had been times when he'd actually felt optimistic. Not overly so, but just enough to get him through the steps they required.

But there were still occasions when Carter didn't think there was a way out, and felt that he was simply biding time until something even more drastic than PTSD invaded his life.

Much of the time his ambivalence defeated him. Or at least set him back a step or two. But always, no matter where he went, when he set that bottle out Carter did so with hope. And, yes, there *was* a tiny thread of it left in him when he cared to look for it. Which he didn't too often. Especially not where Sloane was concerned.

Tonight Carter was restless, in part because of his new life and in part because Sloane was here. Consequently, he paced the dirty hotel room like a caged tiger—back and forth. An hour of it, non-stop, hoping to tire himself out.

But when he stopped he was only physically tired, not emotionally. The thoughts in his brain wouldn't turn off. Thoughts of the two of them, what they'd had, what they'd planned. The big things—talking about having a family, buying a house. The little things—sleeping in late on Sunday mornings, taking walks, bubble baths for two.

"Why?" he whispered, finally sitting down on the edge of the bed, dropping his head into his hands. *"Why?"*

What his cognitive therapy counselor had told him was that there was no answer to *why?* Of course Carter already knew that, because it was the same question so many of his patients asked him. *Why did I get cancer? Why did my daughter die?*

"Instead of asking yourself why it happened, ask yourself how you're going to get through it." That was what the counselor had said.

So how was he going to get through this with Sloane? Minute by minute, hour by hour, day by day? Could he simply ask her to leave and let her know that being anywhere near her scared him more than the bullets had in Afghanistan?

Of course there were no answers popping into his mind. He hadn't expected them to. In fact the only thing in his mind was Sloane. Which meant he needed something to cradle him through the emptiness that was beginning to set in. So it was time to take a ride. That took concentration, and that was what he needed right now. To be concentrating on something other than what wasn't meant to be.

The air was still warm enough outside, even though it was nearing mid-November. And something about being in a place without confines appealed to him. So Carter slipped into his leather jacket, grabbed his helmet and his medical bag, and headed for his motorcycle.

But his phone rang before he reached his motorcycle, and a minute later he was on his way to Red Rock Canyon Resort, where there was an outbreak of food poisoning. Fourteen people down so far.

It actually gave him a little adrenalin rush, having something that would keep him busy coming up. And it made him feel *useful*—which hadn't happened to him in a long, long time.

"Latest count is twenty-one, Doc," reported Paul Jacob, the night manager. He was a nervous, twitchy man, pale and very thin. Tonight, he was so twitchy Carter wondered if he should offer him a sedative.

"What have you been doing with them so far?

"We've been telling them to stay in their rooms, because we don't know if it's contagious, but some of them won't. They keep coming down to the desk, asking for things."

Paul dabbed sweat beads from his brow.

"I've got my night staff out right now, trying to get people back to their rooms so we can keep everything organized, but word is spreading about an illness sweeping through the resort, so I'm afraid some people aren't being so cooperative. A few have even left."

"Well, if it's food poisoning it's probably not contagious, so I'm not too worried about people leaving. And you think it's something from the buffet?" Carter asked.

He didn't often work with sick people since he was—*had been*—a surgeon. He hadn't since his rotation through internal medicine back in med school, so this aspect of medicine was fairly new to him. Food poisoning… There were so many types. He'd spent ten minutes in the parking lot before coming in, reacquainting himself with what he might expect—thank heavens for phones that could browse the internet.

"I've had my staff asking around and there seems to be the one food that's common to all of the people who have complaints. Eclairs. Not sure if that's any help, but—"

"With cream filling?" Carter asked, as an idea began to formulate in his head.

"Yes," Paul said. "Made fresh today. All our pastries are made fresh, with fresh ingredients, so I don't see how—"

"Sneezing, coughing…improper handwashing after sneezing or coughing. Or simply from the skin. That's how it spreads."

If Carter was guessing right, and he was pretty sure he was. "So, the most common symptoms you've seen are vomiting, nausea and stomach cramps?"

Paul nodded.

"And it started shortly after dinner?"

Once again Paul nodded. "You know what it is?"

Carter nodded as well, and half smiled at what was to be his diagnosis. Staphylococcus food poisoning was the fastest-acting food poisoning of all. It could start as soon as thirty minutes after eating contaminated food. Also, the symptoms fitted what Paul had seen.

This type of food poisoning was not often dangerous, unless you were high-risk because of age or another illness. So Carter was keeping his fingers crossed that he was correct.

This kind of food poisoning usually worked its way out on its own in twenty-four hours. His only duty as a doctor would be to address the side issues—especially dehydration. No drugs, and no real treatment unless dehydration became severe.

"Do you have the room numbers and names of everyone who's reported ill?"

"I do—but there may be more who haven't called for a doctor."

"Is there any way for you to check with all your guests to make sure they're OK and see if they need medical attention?"

Carter was worried that someone who was considered high-risk might have collapsed and not be able to report to the front desk.

"Maybe ask everybody to report their status, and if there are any guests who don't have your staff go to check them."

This was a large resort. He'd read in his file that it had four hundred and fifty rooms.

"How many guests do you have registered right now?"

Paul did a quick computer check.

"Close to six hundred. And there are always those who sneak in an extra person or two without registering them, because they think they have to pay extra. Which they don't. One fee accommodates the room's posted capacity and all buffet meals."

He handed a computer printout to Carter.

"These are the names and room numbers of all the guests who've complained so far."

Carter's mind boggled at the number. There were—conservatively—six hundred people in this hotel who might have eaten the eclairs, and yet he could only treat those he knew to be sick. Twenty-one seemed like an unusually low number. Much too low, he decided as he looked over the list of names. There would be more. Many more.

Now his excitement was beginning to change to worry. For he could only treat the symptoms. Tomorrow he'd send samples to the lab and hope for a speedy diagnosis, then deal with that accordingly if something else turned up.

"I need a doctor," a youngish man said, stumbling up to the desk and then practically falling over it. "Bad cramps."

He was pale, quite obviously in distress, and too sick to care that his shoes didn't match and his shirt wasn't buttoned correctly.

"Looks like this is where I start," Carter said, taking hold of the man's arm. "I'm a doctor. How about we go back to your room and I'll have a look at you there?"

Poor guy, Carter thought as he led the man, who said his name was Jeff, to the elevator bank. As illnesses went, this one wasn't serious. But right now Jeff wouldn't believe that.

"So, how many of those eclairs did you eat?" he asked, as he led Jeff onto the elevator.

"A couple." The man moaned. "They were good."

Which meant Carter had his night cut out for him.

A lot of people were sick here. Sloane had heard about it when she'd gone down for a late dinner and the dining room had been closed, with a posted note that food service was suspended until further notice.

They'd left a list of local diners and a pizza delivery

service on the door, but Sloane hadn't been in the mood to go out. And she wasn't a huge fan of pizza.

So she'd grabbed a bag of pretzels from the vending machine, then returned to her room. It didn't matter much to her anyway. Food wasn't her thing. As often as not, since Carter had left, she'd forget to eat a meal and need to be reminded to eat something.

In her defense, it was difficult eating when you didn't have an appetite—which was the case now. But there had been a time when she'd loved to cook for Carter on the days when their schedules had worked out together. Loved the way he'd always created the ambiance, too. Candlelight, wine from one of the local wineries they'd visited—a hobby they'd shared. Dim light. Soft music—Ella Fitzgerald, Frank Sinatra, Nat King Cole… All this, even when the only thing she might have fixed was a simple pasta salad.

He'd been a romantic. Something he'd kept to himself until their fourth or fifth date, when they'd gone to the beach for an evening picnic. Harbor sounds and moonglow over the water…

She knew she'd fallen a little in love with him before that night, but when he'd asked her to dance in the sand with him—that was when he'd won her whole heart. That was the dream that haunted her so often now.

Too many memories, Sloane thought, as she ate the pretzels and then decided to return to the vending machines for a bottle of water, in case what was infecting the guests was waterborne. She didn't want to be sick here. Actually, she didn't know *what* she wanted, other than water, so she slipped back into her shoes and headed to the hall.

Halfway to the elevator, she stopped and watched a familiar figure heading her direction. Practically running.

"You OK?" she asked, noting how frazzled Carter looked.

"Two hours…twenty-six patients."

"With what?"

Carter looked—*animated.* It was the way he'd used to look before a challenging surgery. It was a look she'd liked on him then—and now.

"Some kind of staph bug, I'm guessing. Nothing I can do except tell them they'll be better tomorrow and let them know that if they're not to have the hotel get in touch with me. Also make sure they're not dehydrating."

"No serious consequences?" Sloane asked, taking care not to get too close to him.

Getting close might signal that she had personal intentions of some sort, which she didn't. Why start anything between them if she didn't have to?

"Not yet. Just a lot of people with ruined vacation plans. But I found out there's someone down the hall—Type One diabetes—who's sick. I might have to do some different management. Especially if her blood sugar drops."

"Can I help?" Sloane asked.

"Um…yes. Please," Carter replied, looking stunned by her offer. "If you don't mind?"

They'd never really worked together. Yes, they'd been in the same hospital, often on the same shifts. But never together as a team. And even though she hadn't brought a medical bag on this trip—hadn't expected to do anything medical—Sloane followed Carter to the room, not sure what to make of this.

"Just tell me what you want me to do when we get in there," she said, as Carter raised his fist to knock.

He actually chuckled as a little girl opened the door

to him. "I'd tell you if I knew, but since I haven't treated very many sick people—"

"And you think *I* have?"

"Well, there's nothing like having two eminently qualified surgeons show up to tell you that your illness will run its course in a few hours." He looked down at the girl, who hadn't yet unfastened the door chain. "We're doctors," he said to her. "Did you call the front desk because your mom is sick?"

The girl nodded her head, but still didn't unfasten the chain. "I think my mom's really bad this time," she said. "She ate an éclair, and she's not allowed sugar."

"Could we come in and have a look at her?"

The little girl, who couldn't have been more than ten, looked terrified. "She told me not to open the door to strangers."

"Would you like to look at my medical bag? It will prove I'm a doctor." Carter held it out for her to see, then opened it and let her have a look inside.

Reluctantly the child undid the chain, then stepped away from the door. "My mom's in the bathroom. She's throwing up."

Sloane beat Carter to the bathroom, opened the door and found—

"Call an ambulance!" she shouted out to Carter, who was still busy trying to make the child feel at ease.

By the time he had his phone out Sloane was already on her knees at the woman's side, assessing her pulse.

"Weak, erratic…" She looked at the child, who was now standing behind Carter. "What's your mom's name?" she asked.

"Jeannie," the girl said.

"Jeannie, can you hear me?" Sloane called. Then she looked to Carter. "Can you toss me a blood pressure cuff?" she asked, as he plugged one ear to better hear what she hoped were arrangements for an ambulance.

He nodded, and bent down to his medical bag, which was on the floor at his feet now. He found the digital wrist cuff, then handed it to her. "Ambulance is about an hour out. Maybe a little longer."

"Seriously?" Sloane sputtered, patting Jeannie's cheeks to raise a response. But the woman didn't respond.

"That's the way it is around here. There aren't enough services for the size of the area. According to Matt, it's too spread out. Getting help takes too long."

"Is there any other way to get her to the hospital?" Sloane asked.

"There's a guy who runs a charter helicopter service who will stand in for medical transport when it's needed," Carter said, and he dialed the number he'd stored in his phone earlier while at the same time pulling a blood sugar monitor out of his bag and handing it over to Sloane.

So far he seemed—*good*, she thought. Better than he'd seemed for his last several weeks at the hospital. And while Sloane didn't have time to assess the reasons why, she did acknowledge to herself that this was a little bit of the old Carter showing through. Always collected. Always efficient. Always in charge.

"Jeannie," she said, "if you can hear me, you're going to feel a little pinprick on your finger. I've got to take your blood sugar."

Which was what she did. She drew a drop of blood, let it soak into the test strip, then inserted the strip into the meter. Five seconds later…

"Seven hundred fifty," she whispered, bending down to smell the woman's breath. It smelled like nail polish—a typical smell in ketoacidosis indicating that Jeannie's insulin was too low and her blood sugar too high.

"The helicopter can be here for transportation in fifteen minutes," Carter said, stepping back into the confined space. "Then it will take about forty minutes to get to the largest hospital in the area, or about fifteen to get to the Whipple Creek Clinic."

"She needs to go to hospital," Sloane said without hesitation. "She's got ketoacidosis. Her blood sugar's at seven-fifty."

All which meant there was the possibility of kidney damage or stroke—translating this into a life-threatening situation, especially since Jeannie was comatose.

"Does your mother eat other things she's not supposed to?" Sloane asked the little girl. "And sometimes get very sleepy and sleep for a long time?

"Her name's Molly," Carter said. "Molly McKinley. She's ten and she's in fifth grade. She makes all As, except in math, which she hates, and she makes Bs in that."

"How do you know all that?" Sloane asked, totally surprised by how much he'd interacted with the child when she hadn't been watching. It was the way he'd used to be. Always interacting, always instilling trust. He was so much the old Carter right now she had a hard time remembering him as the Carter he'd turned into.

Carter simply smiled and shrugged. "Guess I just have a way with kids."

Yes, that was the old Carter—*her* Carter. His real smile. His sense of humor. But, as much as she wanted to hope for something more, she couldn't let herself. She'd lost hope months ago, and where Carter was concerned she'd been fighting a daily battle not to let any of it back in. Hope hurt. And she'd already hurt enough. Cried too many tears.

"Anyway, back to your mom," she said, her attention

returning to Molly. "How often does she eat things she's not supposed to?"

"Once a day. She treats herself at night because she doesn't eat anything bad during the day."

So Jeannie was a ritual offender in her diabetic diet. Meaning if she made it through the day without blowing it she'd blow it at night. Also meaning her diabetes was probably never stable.

"How often does she eat bad things other than her nighttime treat?"

"Not as much as she used to. Sometimes two or three times a week."

Here was a brittle diabetic, with food poisoning, comatose from diabetic complications, who, in some way, went off her diet at least once a day. This was serious.

"I think we should get an IV into her," Carter said, pulling himself away from Molly. "I have an idea the food poisoning has only exacerbated an already bad situation. My guess is she was already dehydrated due to her condition, and the food poisoning just stepped it up."

"Do you have something in your medical bag? Because I didn't see…"

"Not in my medical bag. But I have a locked hard bag on my bike that's got a set-up."

His last several words were said on his way out through the door. Which left Sloane there with nothing to do but monitor Jeannie's vital signs. And think about Carter.

Sighing, she looked over at Molly, who was still standing there, wide-eyed. Not sure whether to cry. Not sure what to do. Just like *she'd* been after Carter had left her.

"Come here," she said, patting the spot on the floor next to Jeannie. "Why don't you sit and hold your mom's hand for a little while? I'm sure that's exactly what she'd like right now."

Just as what Sloane would like was her own hand in Carter's—as she'd wanted it for weeks after he'd gone.

CHAPTER FOUR

"IS SHE STABLE?" asked Cruz Montoya as he helped Carter lift Jeannie onto a stretcher.

Cruz owned the helicopter service that hosted tourist rides and doubled as medical transport when it was necessary. Cruz himself was a former Army medic—one who had evacuated patients, who had pulled out dying soldiers under the worst and most dangerous of circumstances.

"No. Her vitals aren't stable and her blood sugar's not responding to insulin yet. There are no signs she's anywhere near coming out of her coma."

"So what about her?" Cruz asked, nodding sideways toward Molly, who'd stepped as far back from the activity as she could. "Is someone going to take care of her?"

"Her grandmother will be here to get her tomorrow, and in the meantime one of the other guests has agreed to watch her. She has three children of her own, and management vouches for her. It's the best we could do under the circumstances."

"Well, if that doesn't work out my mother's here, and I'm sure she'd be glad to look after her for as long as needed."

"I'll keep that in mind," Carter said, looking over at Sloane, who was busy sorting out the oxygen tubing, IV tubing and heart monitor, getting everything ready for transport.

"Can you do this, Carter?" she asked. "The helicopter, I mean?"

It was the same question he'd been asking himself. *Could* he go up in a helicopter? Or even tolerate its noise?

"I guess we're going to find out, aren't we?" he said.

"You don't like choppers?" Cruz asked him.

"And a lot of other things. I took a bad hit in Afghanistan—lots of damage..."

Cruz nodded as if he understood. "Well, I'll try to go easy on you. I had a few quirks when I came back. Glad one of them wasn't flying or else I'd be in real trouble."

"Well, let's hope flying isn't one of mine." Carter grabbed the foot-end of the old-time military stretcher and placed his bag between his patient's feet. "Just letting you know I don't always know what sets me off."

"Are you on a program?" Cruz asked.

"One down in Tennessee. The Recovery Project."

"Where you work with bears?" Cruz asked. "I've heard they have a lot of success. Hope you're one of them."

"You and me, both," Carter said as he helped Cruz load his patient on the helicopter, then climbed in beside her.

He really wanted some diazepam, or something else to calm him down. His pulse was racing faster than he'd ever felt it race. But this was his emergency run, and he wasn't going botch it by either backing out or taking a sedative that at best would make him drowsy and at worst put him to sleep.

"So, how long did you say this trip is going to take?"

"Forty," Cruz said, checking to make sure his passengers were fastened in securely.

"I can do forty," Carter said, hoping that if he sounded confident he would *be* confident.

"That's forty there and forty back. You up to that?"

Carter gulped. Forty minutes seemed like an awfully long time, but eighty…

Face your fears, Holmes.

How many times had he heard those words over the course of the program. Well, if ever there was a fear to face…

"The Recovery Project," Sloane whispered as she searched for it on the internet.

She'd overheard Carter's conversation with the helicopter pilot, and even though he had chosen not to tell her he was in a program, she was curious about it.

Something about bears, the pilot had said. And, sure enough, the project put PTSD patients with rescued baby bears. They took total care of them. Fed them, gentled them, got them ready to turn them loose back into the mountains if their condition warranted it.

It seemed like a good program. Granted, it was an alternative type of treatment, but from what she was reading it incorporated all kinds of PTSD treatment and was especially good at dealing with *acute distress disorder*, which was the type of PTSD Carter was diagnosed with. According to the program's description, it offered factors that office-based therapy and therapy groups could not. One of the primary goals was to allow those with PTSD a safe place to feel and address emotions through the human-animal bond.

Carter and a bunch of bear cubs? The thought of it brought a smile to her face. As improbable as it seemed, Sloane hoped it worked. But why hadn't Carter mentioned that to her? Why couldn't he have trusted her enough to tell her what he was doing? It was a huge step forward for him, and she was proud he was taking it on his own. But she was discouraged that he hadn't included her.

Was it still a trust issue? Had she betrayed his trust in a way she didn't understand?

Even the thought of that caused Sloane's stomach to churn.

Carter hesitated, seeing Sloane sitting in the hotel lobby, waiting for him.

The trip to the hospital and back hadn't been awful. Nothing had triggered him or really got to him at all. Which was a step in the right direction, because so many of his battle casualties had been transported to the hospital by helicopters. Hearing them circle overhead had become a sound he dreaded.

But not tonight. He'd barely noticed, as he'd been focused on his patient, not on himself. Like The Recovery Program had its PTSD victims focus on the bear cubs. A calculated misdirection, he guessed. One that seemed to work. One he hoped would work for him.

Tonight proved that it just might.

"No problems?" Sloane asked, taking the initiative and approaching Carter.

"Everything's fine. I got the patient checked in to Emergency, grabbed a cup of coffee and came right back."

"And the noise of the helicopter didn't—?"

He shook his head. "I'm good. And I appreciate your help."

"I saw four other patients for you while you were gone."

Carter's eyes softened. "Do you realize that stabilizing

Jeannie was the first time we've ever worked together? We were a good team."

Too good. And he hoped that wasn't giving Sloane ideas.

"Anyway, the manager called me on the way in, so I've got another patient to see. Then I think I'm going to hang around here the rest of the night, just in case."

"Does Matt know about the program?" Sloane asked him.

"Yes."

"So it's just me who doesn't know your plans?" she asked.

"We're not together, Sloane. What makes you think I'd want to drag you back into my mess?"

"It's a worthy program, Carter. But I was the one who always searched for the right fit for you, so don't you think I would have been interested in knowing that you're in a program now?"

"I don't know *what* you'd be interested in knowing, Sloane." Carter hated doing this, but she was getting too close again, and in the end that would only hurt her. "And, since we're not together anymore, do you really think I have to tell you everything I do?"

"You never had to do that, Carter. I never asked. I never demanded. When you did tell me, it was because that was what you wanted to do. Not because I was forcing you into it."

Her pain threw him back to all the times before, when they'd had this or similar arguments. It had always triggered him. Any friction with Sloane had triggered him because she'd had him so high on a pedestal he'd always been afraid he'd fall off and disappoint her.

"I know you never tried to force me. But the expectations—"

"Mine or yours?" she asked.

"Both. They were too much. I couldn't stand up to them—even when you were telling me you knew I could do it. Sometimes I could, but sometimes I couldn't, and I didn't know how to deal with that—especially when something was triggering me."

Namely, *her*. Knowing how disappointed she would be if he failed had been a trigger. Knowing how much he was hurting her had been a trigger. Also coming to terms with the fact that he couldn't take care of Sloane the way he needed to had been a trigger. And all the triggers had added up to one big failure, and that had been the biggest trigger of all—failing Sloane.

"Have you ever just tried to work through one of those moments? I know when you were back at the hospital you didn't turn away from anything. But the longer you stayed there, the more you seemed to doubt yourself. Was it something I did, Carter? Or something I didn't do? Because if that's the case—"

He cut her off with the wave of his hand. "Look, would you care to go to the lounge for a drink? Maybe sit down and sort through some things."

She raised her eyebrows. "The lounge? Is that still the way you fix everything? With alcohol?"

"Wine for you…a nice Chablis. And fizzy water with lime for me. Sometimes it's not easy, but it's one demon on a long list I *can* control."

"That's great! You know what they say about little steps and how they turn into big ones. You always were disciplined when you set your mind to it. So, what about the—well—you know. You were smoking a lot of—pot. Taking a lot of pills. Oh, and I'll take a fizzy water as well. Going night hiking in a while and I want to be clear-headed."

"Good thinking on the water. And as for the pot and pills—three months off that, too. I'm working it out as well."

"Excellent, Carter. Especially since you're taking these steps on your own. A lot of people don't have that kind of determination. And I'm also happy to hear The Recovery Project is working for you. It should give you hope for much more progress. I'm really hopeful, too. Because maybe, somewhere down the line, we can be friends again. I know the rest of it's over, but I always did value your friendship."

"I'm keeping my fingers crossed for a lot of things, Sloane."

But for them? He wasn't ready to go that far. He'd done too much damage. He'd hurt her too much. And he didn't trust himself enough yet to think he could, or even deserved to have Sloane back in his life.

Carter looked up at the chandelier in the lobby. A thousand crystals glittered overhead, looking like little bits of shattered mirrors, reflecting everything around it. That was how he felt. Shattered. And with so many things reflecting him.

"I may not have all the answers, and God knows there are a lot of things I can't control, but there are some things I can. And what I need to do is to get through this program and see what happens after that."

"Like becoming a full-fledged bear rescuer?"

He chuckled. "Possibly. Being a GP wasn't what I had in mind when I went to medical school, but here I am—so who knows?"

"If that's what you want, Carter, you should go after it. Whatever makes you happy. Because I think the happier you are, the better your PTSD will get."

Carter could almost envision the two of them, living

in a mountain cabin, running their own rescue. Maybe even developing a PTSD program to go with it. The lifestyle would be different from anything he'd ever thought about, but it would be good. Only with Sloane, though. And since there *was* no Sloane in his life now that dream disappeared almost at the same time it appeared.

"I still like being a doctor," he said. "But at least with a bear you don't get someone who purposely destroys their health by going against their doctor's order the way Jeannie does."

They went to the lounge, ordered fizzy water, then talked for a while longer. It was mostly about friends and incidental things. Nothing heavy, nothing about his illness. Nothing about what they had or what they'd lost. Oh, did you know Mrs. Levy's poodle had puppies? By the way, there's a new bakery down on Mulberry Street. They have great pastries. It wasn't as easy as he would have liked, but it wasn't nearly as awkward as he'd expected it to be. Surprisingly, the time passed quickly, maybe too quickly, and all too soon Sloane was scooting toward the edge of her seat.

"Look, I know you're back on duty now, but I do have a couple patients I promised to check in on before my hike. So if you don't mind…?"

"Not at all. Besides, I've got a couple to see myself, then I'm going to try and get back to my room for a quick shower and a nap before I have to come back here to do some rechecks. So, when did you get interested in night hiking? I remember we used to talk about it, but you were never as keen as I was."

"Since I got here. It's amazing how the desert literally springs to life at night. The stars, the animals, the feeling that you're the only one in the universe…"

Sloane smiled.

"It's something new for me, discovering things on my own. Usually you were the one doing the discovering and I was the one who tagged along. But this is different. It's mine. And it's really exciting because they've put me in a small advanced group. Anyway, since I'll be out, why don't you use my room here and save yourself the trouble of going home and then returning."

She fished the key card from her pocket and handed it to him.

"I'll just let the day clerk know where you'll be—unless you want to do that yourself?"

He drew in a deep breath and let it out slowly, as the mere brush of her hand on his sent tingles up his spine.

"Are you sure you want me there? Because it seems like I would be taking advantage, in case you did want to return for any reason."

As he handed her back the card, Carter pulled his hand away from hers a little more slowly than would be strictly called for. But, even in that little touch, so many memories had sprung up—good memories—he was reluctant to break the contact because in that moment, they were the way they used to be. Nothing had changed them, nothing had separated them. But that was only a fantasy, and as he broke the sensation that was trying to overtake him, the memories vanished, and they returned to being the same Sloane and Carter they were now.

"I might go rifling through your things."

She laughed.

"I have the same old things I had when we were together. I haven't been in the mood to buy myself anything new, so feel free to rifle."

He studied her for a moment. She was so beautiful, yet he could see the worry in her eyes. He'd put it there, even after all the times he'd told her not to worry, that he could take care of himself. Which, he couldn't, and that was painfully obvious. Then there was that cycle, the more obvious he became, the more she worried. Round and round, like a carousel he couldn't get off. Until the day he did.

"I'm not sure we should be doing this," he said.

"Doing what?"

"Trying so hard. Like you said, we need to take baby steps leading to bigger ones. I don't want to go back to the place where you tried to take care of me and I resisted just about everything you did."

He couldn't return to those awful months where she had tried so hard to help him that he had felt trapped. He knew it was because she cared, but what he knew and what he felt were two different things.

"It was smothering, Sloane. Not that you meant to do that, but I was so resistant that any attempt to help me seemed like I was being smothered. And it wasn't just you. It was all those counselors early on. They didn't have the right things to offer me. Not then. But what my counselor told me was that it was just me, not being ready to admit all the things I'd eventually have to admit. One being that you weren't really smothering me; I was smothering myself in pity and all kinds of other emotions I couldn't yet face."

"I never meant to do that, Carter, and I'm sorry that's what it felt like to you. Why didn't you say something?"

"Because I wasn't saying much of anything. How could I, when I didn't even know who I was anymore? Sometimes it just seemed easier to go along and hope I didn't mess things up too badly."

"And I was left imagining all sorts of things since you wouldn't tell me, then trying to put all the pieces of your jigsaw puzzle together. But you were getting farther and farther away from me, and I was trying everything I could think of to help you. Even though nothing was working."

"Why did you stay, Sloane? Why weren't you the one to leave?"

"Because every now and then I'd catch a glimpse of you, and that gave me hope. I loved you, Carter. I didn't want to give up because I thought you needed me. Or because I wanted you to need me. But I was wrong about that, too, wasn't I?"

"Maybe you were, at least toward the end. I'm sorry about that, but because I didn't know who I was anymore, there was no way you could have known. And maybe I was angry with you for that. Maybe I expected, or assumed, you, of all people, should know who I was," he said, feeling like a louse.

"The truth is, I don't know what was motivating me at that point. Frustration. Anger. Fear. Maybe some self-loathing. Could be I was trying to prove I was still me, even when I knew I wasn't. The worst part was hearing myself saying something hurtful to you, and not being able to control it. But, I couldn't stop myself. Because you were always there, you turned into my target."

"I knew it was. And often the only thing that kept me sane through it all was knowing that the Carter I fell in love with wouldn't have done that. It was all I had to hold on to."

She was right. The real Carter *wouldn't* have done that to her. But the real Carter hadn't come home from Afghanistan and he wouldn't. In a sense he had died there, and the Carter who had taken his place wasn't the man Sloane had fallen in love with.

"Anyway, about your room…"

"The offer's still open and you don't have to read anything into it. I was only trying to make the next few hours a little easier on you. Take it or leave it."

"Sorry I overreacted," he said. "And I do appreciate the offer, but I need to stop by my office to see a few late-night patients after I'm done here, then after that I think I'll just go back to my room."

He looked longingly at the key card, now in Sloane's hand, and wished he could take it, with or without strings. But, that's not where he was, or even anywhere close to where he should be. She was too tempting, even with such an innocent gesture, and he had to be careful not to give in. Not to persuade himself that just this one time…

Carter slid out of the booth after Sloane but followed her out of the lounge rather than walking with her.

"I still don't get a lot of things right," he said, once they were in the lobby.

She smiled half-heartedly, then nodded.

"No big deal. This isn't easy and neither of us is winning any awards for getting it right. But I really am excited by your progress, Carter. No matter what else happens between us, I want you to succeed probably as much as you do. I always have."

"Trust me. A checkmark in the win tally of my life is a lot of incentive. I don't have too many of those on there yet, but I'm not giving up."

He reached over and took hold of her hand, and squeezed it, "Promise."

"I'll hold you to it," she said, squeezing back.

"I hope you do."

And he meant it. Even if they couldn't be who they used to be, maybe they could have something else. He hoped so, because not having Sloane in his life left him with a great big hole in his heart.

His whole objective at one in the morning had used to

be drinking enough to pass out. That had been his normal in the past. Now he didn't *have* a normal. He took it as it came—whatever it was—and struggled through the best way he could.

In a few minutes the struggle would be with Sloane. He wanted to be near her so badly, even though he knew he shouldn't. But his impulses sometimes still took control, and Sloane was an impulse that he couldn't cure easily.

"So, how were your patients?" Carter asked a little while later, as she passed in the hall.

"Everything's fine. Everybody recovering quite nicely. I'll get my patient notes to you later, if that's OK?"

"No need to rush. My receptionist doesn't transcribe, and it takes me forever to get everything recorded, so I'm really not in a hurry."

Sloane laughed. "She really didn't impress me as a good fit for a medical practice."

"But she comes with the office," Carter said. "One of those buy-one-get-one offers. And I may not be here much longer than two months anyway, so I can cope with her."

"Two months?"

"Then on to my bears. It's the second part of the program. We get all the teaching during the first part, and start on the path to recovery. Then they give you a short reprieve, to see if you're responding well enough to the program or lagging behind so much you have to repeat the first part of your therapy. They want to make sure you're ready for each step you're supposed to accomplish so they can recognize and respond to issues they don't know about. A lot of people with PTSD cover up certain aspects of it, and the counselors at The Recovery Project expect that and prepare for it."

"And they're watching you right now?"

"Not directly. This is my time to see if I can work through what I learned in the first part of the program. But I do call my counselors twice a day. If they think I'm having problems they can't work through long distance, or if I think I'm having problems, they'll call me back to Tennessee to see what I need. It's a tight program. A lot of it's based on faith in yourself, but most of it's based on trust."

"Sounds like you're really sold on it."

"I am, because I'm hoping I can come back here and practise when I'm through it. Maybe buy my part of the practice from Matt. Somewhere in the future see what I can set up here to help other people with PTSD problems. Forgeburn has a lot of potential, with its wide-open spaces. It's a great place to get away and discover yourself, and if it works out for me here, it should work for others."

"And Matt's OK with you leaving in a few weeks?"

"He's great about it. In fact, he's excited for me He's going to do some kind of co-operative exchange with the Whipple Creek Clinic to make sure he's covered. I mean it, this is the place I want to start over, Sloane. It's not what I had before, but it's what I need now. Something simpler and scaled back. A chance to breath. And, heal."

"I guess I expected you to come back to Manning Hospital if you returned to medicine. But this sounds good, Carter. It sounds as though you've made some excellent plans for your future, and I'm excited for you."

"Thank you," he said simply. "It's going to take a while, but I've got all the time in the world so, as we've been saying, baby steps…"

"Do you think you'll ever return to surgery?" she asked.

"Not in the immediate future. I think the stress of it is part of what triggers me, and my counselors are telling me I must keep my stress levels down. So, it's not in my plans right now, and I have no idea about the future."

"You know Daddy will always take you back don't you? If you get through your program and decide you want to go back."

Carter knew she meant well. She always had, and he deeply appreciated it. But going back to where he had been? That wasn't going to happen because his life was about moving forward now.

"Tell him thank you for me and that if I want to be a surgeon again, I've got a long way to go to get there. Right now, it's just not my aim, but Forgeburn is. So, I hope he's not holding my position open hoping that, by some miracle, I'll come walking through the hospital door one day, cured and ready to take up surgery again. Because, nothing's going to cure me, Sloane. I can be helped and taught to take better control of myself and my life. But I'm fighting a lifelong sentence, and I can't predict any outcomes for myself. That's one thing I've learned in surgery. Work with where you are today and don't plan too diligently for the future because you're in transition and things will change."

"You've come a long way in three months, Carter. I hope we can maintain some kind of relationship, so I can see where you're going because I'm really happy about your progress. I only wish I'd found better help for you months ago, so you could have been on your way sooner, and I'm sorry I didn't. But it's all good now, and I'm confident it's going to work for you, especially seeing how far you've come."

He hoped she meant that. But right now, she seemed so lost, he wasn't sure. And it was his fault. Every ounce of sadness and doubt he saw in Sloane was what he'd put there. For that, he was truly sorry. And that, above all else, was why he'd left.

It broke his heart seeing the results of his handiwork, and for Sloane to put any part of that behind her, he had to leave. Had to give her a fresh start. It had never been because he didn't love her. He did when he'd rode away. And still did, now.

But could he ever really love her the way he had? Totally, completely. Especially knowing what his love had cost her? Would it be better to hang back, or pull away altogether? And could she ever love him the way she had, especially after she'd stepped into the role of caregiver of sorts?

The answers weren't clear. And, they weren't easy, not for either of them. Their love had changed, and nothing was going to be the same. But, could it work differently?

"It hasn't been easy, but I'm optimistic the outcome will be better than what I have going for me now."

"That's all I ever wanted for you," Sloane said. "And I suppose I thought I was helping you."

"You were—by being there. I needed you there, Sloane. Supporting me, but not trying to cure me. That's my battle, and the only way I can win it is if I figure out the strategies by myself."

They stepped outside to the veranda and sat on a stone wall overlooking a meticulously-sculpted desert garden with pink-blooming prickly pear cacti, scarlet hedgehog cacti and Joshua trees. The colors, even in the dim lights on the pergola next to them, were breathtakingly vibrant, and his gaze fixed on another couple, walking along the edge of the garden, holding hands, so absorbed in each other there was nothing else in their world. He and Sloane had been that way once, but now, in the dimming of the day, they sat separated by too much distance, physically and emotionally, and he didn't know how to repair it.

"I'm here, Sloane, because I was worried about slipping back into old patterns that exacerbated my PTSD. The way you worried made my anxiety worse because I didn't like seeing you suffer. And I didn't want you worrying about me all the time. Watching. Waiting. Trying to anticipate what I might do next, when that's something that can't be anticipated. It wouldn't have worked for us. In fact, in the long run, I think it would have destroyed both of us. And, you didn't deserve what my illness was doing to you. I couldn't watch that, and there were so many times seeing how you suffered caused my anxiety to increase because there was nothing I could do to help you."

"Did I ever complain, Carter? Did I ever say anything that led you to believe that I didn't want to help you through this?"

"You didn't have to say anything," he countered. "I knew you, and I could see how I was affecting you. I could see how nervous you were becoming, see the distractions you were experiencing at work because of me. I was putting you at risk, Sloane. In your personal life and worse, in your job as a surgeon. Most of all, I could see it in your eyes, the way you looked at me, the way you struggled to be patient when I knew you wanted to scream or kick something."

He reached over and took hold of her hand, then scooted just a little closer.

"In the state I was in, I couldn't stay there and let it keep happening over and over, so I left. And I'm so sorry that's what I had to do, but my life was closing in on me. I knew I was getting to my now-or-never point."

"But, the way you left..."

"It was bad form, and I regret it. But I debated a clean break versus something long and drawn out. And if it had come to long and drawn out, I don't think I could have left you. Not if you cried, or held on to me, or simply asked. At that time, Sloane, I wasn't strong enough to do anything other than what I did. So, I suppose I chose what most would consider the coward's way out, but it's what I thought was best for both of us."

"It wasn't best for me, Carter. You did what you thought was best for you, and you didn't even tell me what was happening, or how you were feeling. We might have been able to work out some of the problems differently than we did but you didn't give us a chance, and after so many years..."

Now there were tears in her eyes. He was making her cry again, like the many times she'd hidden herself away from him and cried. He'd heard her. And now, he saw her. But he wasn't sure he was ready to face the way he hated what he always seemed to do to her.

"Look, I—I um—"

To hell with what he needed. Sloane's needs came first. They always had because that's the way he'd always wanted it. Sloane before him. At least prior to his PTSD. Then he'd done selfish things. A few at first, like missing a meal when he knew she'd cooked for him or staying out later than he'd told her he would, which he knew it would cause her to worry. Eventually, it turned into the bigger things—staying out all night, the addictions that were getting closer to being out of control. That's when he'd shoved Sloane behind him. That's when he actually believed he owed it to himself to come first in everything. His way, or no way.

But now… Carter moved closer to Sloane and pulled her into his arms as she cried. Quiet sobs on his shoulder. And he held her, stroked her hair, rocked her gently.

"I wasn't able to work out anything by the time I finally left," he told her. "But, it was me, not you. Never you, Sloane, and I should have told you that much, tried to make you understand. By the time I left though, I'd already lost me. At least the good parts of me who knew what I was leaving behind. The rest of me—it didn't really matter."

She sniffled but didn't pull away from him.

"You always mattered, Carter. The good, the bad—sure, I was struggling, but there was never a moment you didn't matter. Until I received your text message. Then I was left wondering what I was doing, and why I wasn't the one leaving you. I had cause, you didn't. But I couldn't walk away, and it wasn't even because I loved you. And I did. It was because I thought I could help. I truly believed my feelings for you would be part of your cure. I was wrong, though. Wasn't I?"

He loved her so much he'd had to walk away. She'd loved him so much she'd had to stay.

"I honestly don't know if you were wrong, or not."

She finally pushed away from him, the wiped the remaining tears with the back of her hand, then sniffed.

"It shouldn't have been such a mess. But it was too complicated, and overwhelming, going from a life that made sense to one that didn't. And we did make sense, Carter. Even now, with all you've been through, and with the way our feelings have changed, you know we made sense."

"Once upon a time," he said, with a wistful sigh.

"Once upon a time without the happily-ever-after ending. Shouldn't stories like ours have a happy ending?"

"I used to think so, but after what I saw when I was in the Army, and after what I went through—too many people never get their happily-ever-after ending."

He stared at her face for a moment. A bit red, a bit blotchy. But so beautiful he ached from the memories of when that face radiated happiness and joy. Then, but not now.

"Look, it's getting late and I've got a couple of late-nighters coming to the office, so I need to get going. If we need to talk some more..."

"Not now," she said, looking up at him. "Like I said earlier, I'm signed up for that night hike and it's about time for me to go. So, I don't want to talk anymore right now, Carter, because I've got to figure out where all of this is going."

She stood up, too, then took three steps forward and placed a soft kiss on Carter's cheek—an old habit she didn't want to break. And she didn't care if she should, because it was the only reminder from their past that transcended their problems and, for that instant, carried them back to when their life together good.

"Once upon a time," she whispered, then walked away.

Carter watched her until she joined up with her group of hikers on the other side of the desert garden. No matter what it took, he wasn't going to hurt her again, even if he had to run to a place where he could lose himself forever, if that's what Sloane needed. Putting her first again—it's what he had to do even though the outcome would not be what he wanted. But when you loved someone they way he loved Sloane...

CHAPTER FIVE

CARTER LOOKED LIKE HELL. After a long night, followed by a long day, he felt like it, too. Four more re-checks at the hotel and an unexpectedly long queue of patients waiting at his office until halfway through the night, and he was officially exhausted. And grungy. And filled with a fast flurry of thoughts that simply wouldn't go away. All that, plus his back hurt. Maybe he'd pulled a muscle? Or bumped into something that, by morning, would be a nice purple bruise. Whatever the reason, he just wanted to take his aches and pains and go to sleep. Except, when he tried, sleep rejected him. Caused him to pace the room, then take a couple of acetaminophen for his back, hoping a little bit of over-the-counter relief would finally let him put his head down on the pillow and close his eyes.

Acetaminophen. Such a mild relief for a man who'd been addicted to morphine when he was in the hospital, and anything he could get when he was out. But, it was all he allowed himself, even though a few of his back twinges were beginning to kick him a little harder than he cared for. Which meant it was time to force himself into some kind of relaxation to allow the spasms to subside. Physician, heal thyself. Yeah, right. There were just too many things to heal so he was just taking them one by one rather than overwhelming himself.

Of course, as spasms went, what he was having now wasn't severe. Not like when he'd been injured, anyway. He'd had a stage five nephrology injury, the worst of the worst. It had been a shattered kidney, excruciatingly torn from its pedicle—basically what had attached his kidney to him. So, he'd had to lose one kidney. And have some surgical repair to the other. Not as excruciating, but painful all the same. Then had come the nephrologist's pep talk. A lot of people lived a normal, productive life with only one.

Yeah, right. Normal and productive.

All that, and he'd hardly even noticed they'd removed his spleen. Sure, he'd removed dozens of spleens and sure, he'd been the one giving the pep talks. It's nice to have a spleen, but not necessary. Then the "normal and productive life" malarkey.

What goes around comes around, Carter supposed, as he looked at himself in the mirror and frowned. He needed sleep. A shower to try and ward off the building anxiety, then at least four hours of hibernation before he started all over again. Also, he couldn't afford any more thoughts about Sloane—they weren't conducive to shutting his eyes and hoping visions of sugarplums were strong enough to fight their way in.

But that wasn't happening. Not in the shower. Not in his bed. Not in the rickety, revolting chair next to the bed—the one he'd thrown a sheet over, so he didn't have to touch the chair's fabric. The more he fought it, the more his anxiety crept in. If he went to sleep now, he could still get in four hours…three hours…two hours.

What would have happened, he wondered, if he had taken Sloane up on her offer of her room? Or maybe he had subconsciously hoped she'd come back? Or had he simply liked the idea that he was sleeping in her bed, with his head on her pillow?

If that was the case, his diagnosis would have been he was still in love with her. And not in the "fond friend" kind of way, but in every sense of the word. Not that he didn't already know that.

"Well?" Carter asked the mirror as he started to pace again, knowing if he went to sleep right now, he'd only get one hour "Are you, or aren't you?"

He didn't want to do so much as even think the answer because, if he did, he might have to do something about it.

"What? Try to win her back?"

That question came with another scary answer. Sloane still loved him. There was no denying that. And if Carter fell into that, took a sidestep away from his promise not to involve her again, he'd be back at the beginning.

Love didn't change everything in his case. In fact, it made things worse. Thank God, some reason had latched on to him because while yes, he did want to win her back, he knew he couldn't do it. He wasn't ready. And Sloane wasn't over what he'd done to her before.

Then, there was the fundamental issue of how she triggered him because he hated what he was doing. He was traveling down a crooked path, and love was hard to sort when PTSD was hanging on for that journey.

"And there you have your answer," Carter said, then backed away, grabbed up his shirt, put it on and headed for the door. Maybe he'd have an early breakfast, or simply take a walk. Either way, it was better than what he was going through in his room—his isolated, cockroach-ridden little room.

Who was it that said something about how, if you loved something, you should set it free? He didn't remember the entirety of the quotation, but he did understand the drift of it. Since he loved Sloane, and he wasn't good for her, it was time to let go.

"Damn," Carter said, heading to his motorcycle.

Why did it always have to be so difficult? Why did his feelings for her make him ache so badly?

Because what he wanted, and what he got to have, were two entirely separate things. That's why.

Shuffle your thoughts, Carter warned himself. It was a tip he'd picked up from his counselor on what to do when he knew he was getting too close to his anxiety limit. Think of something else. Redirect his attention.

Which is what he did now. He pulled out his phone and looked at his calendar for the day. Six patients scheduled in the office this morning, and two outside. Not bad, he thought. The only problem was, he had two hours before anybody in Forgeburn stirred. Which meant he had time to kill, and empty time was his worst enemy.

As often as not, when he wasn't occupied, the whole overthinking process would start, then something he didn't want to think would squeeze its way in and eventually take over.

Sighing, he was feeling his lack-of-sleep hangover. Thankfully, his back spasms had let up, which was a good thing, otherwise he wouldn't have been able to climb on his bike and head over to the Red Rock Inn for a morning coffee and a cloak-and-dagger glimpse of Sloane. But, by the time he got there, and found a seat at the counter in the hotel's all-night diner, it was too late. Sloane had beaten him there, she was right by the entrance where she couldn't miss him. And, she didn't.

"You up early, or haven't you gone to bed?" she asked him, heading to the counter to order a latte rather than taking a seat next to him in the blue and brown-striped banquette that ran the length of the tiny diner.

"A little of both, I suppose. If you don't sleep all night, then it only serves to reason that you're getting up early."

Sloane was too bright-eyed from her overnight expedition. Too animated.

"Did you have a good time?" he asked her, even though the look on her face told him she'd loved every minute of it. Why did he have to know her so well?

"There were three of us, plus the guide, and we got into some really nice areas. We heard coyotes. We didn't get close enough to disturb them, but we could see the glow of their eyes. The air and the ground temperature were cool, which was nice, since we covered nearly ten miles. And there were so many different little night creatures out there: mammals, birds, insects that hide during the day. Oh, and the reptiles—there were so many of them scattered around, looking for a rock that still maintained some daytime heat. When they got warm enough they went off in search of a meal… It was absolutely breathtaking how much goes on in the more remote areas at night. I'm hoping I got some good photos, because we encountered an enormous variety of nocturnal life—like snakes, skunks, scorpions, kangaroo rats, jack rabbits, owls, and even a bobcat."

"You weren't in any danger, were you?" Carter asked.

Even though she'd been with other people, he worried because he knew what Sloane was like. She got excited, and ignored everything but what she was focused on. Like the time he'd taught her how to mountain bike. She'd taken three detours into the dirt because she had been so distracted by how she pedaled, she'd forgotten to watch where she pedaled. Eventually, it always came together, but in the new undertakings in her life, Sloane's excitement too often overshadowed her abilities. So, yes, he worried. He always worried about her. He couldn't help himself.

"No. Our guide gave us some basic rules to follow and told us if we didn't do exactly what he said we'd have to go back to the resort." Sloane paused for breath, then continued, the flush of excitement still rosy on her cheeks. "I wish you could have been there, Carter. You would have loved it."

"Maybe next time," he said, even though he knew there wouldn't be a next time.

"You look…terrible," Sloane said, in her usual morning-perky voice.

She had always been a morning person. He'd been the one who'd thought the only reason to have a morning was to sleep through it.

"You don't like the new look?" Carter said, looking down to check that he'd put on fresh clothes after his shower, since he'd been too groggy to really notice. Luckily he was good. Or at least his clothes were.

"What I don't like is the way *you* look, and it has nothing to do with your clothes."

"Being tired will do that to you."

He watched her pick up her to-go latte, then walk over to his table. She was hesitant, like she wasn't sure if she wanted to be involved with him this early or would rather put it off until later. Or, never.

"Which is why I'm going into my office early, hoping I can grab some sleep before I start seeing patients."

"Later, I'd like to show you something."

He raised a weary, yet very wicked eyebrow.

"Really?"

Sloane laughed.

"Not *that*. But earlier, up on Flat Top—it's a rock formation rock formation we came through a little while ago—there was a herd of desert bighorn sheep emerging, but we didn't have time to stop and take pictures so I thought if you had some free time maybe we could go up there together. The hike's not very impressive considering where we used to go, but the view… I can see why you like Forgeburn. If I weren't so city I might move here just for the view"

She held up her camera, then asked. "Want to come with me?"

"Right after lunch?" he asked, surprised, yet pleased, she'd asked him. "Unless there's an emergency, my afternoon is free."

Her smile was so big and bright he couldn't turn her down. Never had been able to, when she looked at him that way.

"So how far is this Flat Top?"

"Just a couple of miles. The hiking trail is a little advanced, for most of the people here, but the guide said there were a couple of rough ones in the area, so I'm hoping to see what they're about. Maybe you'd like to hike along with me for that, as well."

Hiking was one of the many things they'd been good at. Hiking someplace out of the way, finding a secluded spot, making love in the open air. That had been very good, as well.

"Just let me know when you want to go, and if I'm free…"

He shrugged. This was a dangerous idea. Too many reminders. Too much of their past inching back in. But before his illness, he'd never been able to say 'no' to Sloane and, apparently, that was also inching back in, as well.

Carter seemed rested, but restless. Sloane could tell from the way he lagged back. And sure, asking him to come with her probably wasn't the best idea she'd ever had. But she'd remembered the way they used to get so excited when they discovered something new in their journeys, and before she knew it, the invitation had slipped out. So here they were, looking for sheep, and Carter had barely spoken a word since they'd left the hotel. Getting some sleep might have improved his physical condition, but his mind wasn't here.

"You OK?" she finally asked, after they had hiked almost a mile in silence.

"Just weighing some options. Nothing to worry about."

"Anything you want to tell me?" she asked, as they stopped for a few minutes to have some water and a regroup.

"Not really. I was thinking ahead to what life is going to be like living here."

"And…?"

"And I think it's going to be good. I'm not sure I'm meant to live in the city anymore. It's too—confining."

"Is that your PTSD talking, or you?"

"A little of both, I suppose. My PTSD put me in the position to find something new, and I like what I've found. Sometimes isolation is good."

"But do you want to stay this isolated for the rest of your life?"

"What I want for the rest of my life is to be able to count on myself, and if I can do that here, in the desert, this is where I want to be."

For a city girl, Sloane had been surprised how much she had enjoyed the desert, too. It was something she could get used to, but so far Carter had made no mention of her staying here. She had listened to him very closely, hoping to hear something that would encourage her, but every time he had got near something that sounded like the possibility of hope for them, he had backed away from it. Maybe that was for the best, though, as she was changing, just like he was, and maybe the person she'd turn into wouldn't be the woman who had once loved him to distraction. She hoped that wasn't the case, but she couldn't count it out.

"It's a good place, and if it's what you need, I'm happy for you."

But not for herself as, now, Sloane was facing the same dilemma he was. Where was she supposed to be, and was it with, or without Carter?

As they approached the narrowing of the trail she spotted a little Gila monster, out sunning itself on a rock. It was watching them warily, probably not wanting to give up its place in the sun. She didn't blame the creature. The sun here was glorious. And the air so clean, and the sky so blue. Normally, she didn't notice these things, but now that she had, she wondered if it had something to do with what could be emerging as a desire to stay here with Carter? Not that he'd asked her, and not that she expected him to. But still, is that what she wanted? Was her subconscious directing her in a way her consciousness was still resisting?

"They're venomous," Carter said. "Beautiful though."

"But not deadly."

"It's a hell of a bite if it gets you. It kind of chews its way into your skin then hangs on for dear life. Leaves you with a neurotoxin that's going to hurt. The bite area's going to be afflicted with edema and you're going to get weak because your blood pressure will drop critically. Just saying…"

"It's a hell of a bite if you let it bite you. But it's such a slow mover you'd have to be an idiot not to get out of its path."

Sloane pointed her camera at the creature, who'd yet to move, and shot several photos. Then she stomped on the ground and laughed as the lazy lizard finally decided to waddle away.

"See how it runs," she said, looking back at Carter, who was stretched out on a large rock, sunning himself much the way the Gila monster had been. He was breathing a little too hard, she thought. But maybe he still wasn't in the best of shape.

She snapped some photos of him, then returned to the path.

"You can stay there if you want. But that rattler sneaking up behind you might have some different ideas about what it wants to do with your rock."

That was all it took for Carter to jump up, then spin around to look for the snake.

"There's no rattlesnake here," he said.

"But there could have been."

They'd always played little jokes on each other. It had been part of the dynamic between them she'd loved. And, while she hadn't meant to do it, it had come naturally. Sloane didn't regret it, though, because just for that moment it was nice getting that little piece of them back.

"And you, Sloane Manning, are a wicked woman."

Carter caught up to her just as the trail narrowed to barely allow one person through and grabbed hold of her. He spun her around to face him. Then smiled.

"Stand back, woman, while I take the lead."

"For fifty feet," Sloane said, pointing ahead to a big red rock that definitely had a flat, tabletop appearance. "That's our destination."

"And no sheep in sight," Carter said, squeezing past her.

For that instant, when their bodies pressed together,

Sloane held her breath. It felt so good, having him that close. His body squeezed tight to hers. So many memories came flooding back, of all the times when a simple movement like that had started something more.

"Oh, there will be sheep," she said, practically forcing the words out of her mouth. His effect on her was so strong she was almost dizzy with it.

Carter paused briefly, still pressed to her, and studied her face the way he'd done so many times before. He'd claimed it was because he could read her. Maybe he could. Or maybe he wanted to. Whatever the case, she couldn't look him in the eye. He might see things he wasn't meant to. Things she'd put away, or was trying to put away. Things that still hung on. He didn't need to know any of that. Didn't have that right any more.

So Sloane looked off to the side, taking great care not to make direct contact lest his siren effect would lure her in. She was already a wreck and she didn't need to deal with any more of that. Even though she still loved him.

But it was a dangerous love now, because it hurt so much.

"Lead on," she said finally, squirming away from him.

"We were good, like you said before," Carter said before he turned back to the trail. "I'm sorry I destroyed it."

"We both destroyed it," Sloane said. "You by pushing me away, and me by not recognizing when I needed to step away and let you lick your own wounds."

She fell into line behind Carter but kept her eyes on the red dirt trail.

"Neither of us got it right."

He stopped and spun to face her so abruptly she bumped into him.

"You have no blame in this, Sloane. I did what I did because I couldn't control myself. Not my actions, not my thoughts. That's where it started, and anything that came after was simply a reaction."

"I loved you so much, Carter..." Sloane said, and tears started slipping down her cheeks.

Carter brushed them back with his thumb and gently pulled her into his chest.

"I know you did," he said, so quietly it was barely more than a whisper. "And you were all I thought about while I was in Afghanistan. All I wanted was to come home to you. But I never came home."

Sloane sniffled, then looked up at Carter. His eyes were so distant. He was staring at—nothing. It was such a sad sight she almost couldn't bear to look at him.

"Why did you go?" she asked him. "Your career was set. You were getting some amazing offers from hospitals all over the country. Then one day you came home and simply said you'd joined the Army. But you wouldn't tell me why, except to say it was something you had to do—your patriotic duty. Why did you have to do it, Carter? I have a right to know, since you came back so broken. It was an honorable thing to do, and I was proud of you. But the cost was so high and I never really understood why you broke us apart to do it."

Carter took Sloane's hand and pulled her away from the narrow path to an area that opened up into a wide expanse of red rocks and desert plants, then motioned for her to sit down on a rock next to him.

"I never told you because—because I wasn't sure you'd understand."

He took hold of her hand and kissed her open palm, the way he'd always done.

"And you're right. You do have the right to know. It was an obligation I had to fulfill for someone I loved deeply."

"Another woman?" she asked.

There had been other women in Carter's past. She knew that and it didn't bother her, because he'd always been honest about it. But another woman who had the kind of influence it would take to persuade him into joining the Army? And at a time when their first anniversary of being together was coming up?

"Who was she?"

"He. Who was *he*? And *he* was my brother. You remember me telling you about James?"

"He died young didn't he? Cystic fibrosis?"

Carter had never really said much about James and she had always sensed that the loss was still painful, even after all these years. So, she'd never asked him much. At least nothing she'd thought would bring up sad memories for him.

"James was two years younger than me and he was sick. As you know the CF was very progressive with him, and we always knew he wouldn't be with us for very long. But it never stopped us from including him in all our family activities. He was such a—a vital force. Always happy. Always the one to cheer us up when we were down or worried about him."

Carter sniffed, then wiped away the tears forming in his eyes.

"One of the things he always talked about was growing up and joining the Army. My dad was a career Army man, and James wanted to be just like him. Of course we knew that wouldn't happen, but it meant so much to him—especially when Dad would let him wear one of his uniform hats. Anyway, I made a promise to James that I'd become a doctor when I grew up, and then I'd find or invent something to cure him, so he could go in the Army. He believed me. But he was only seven, and most seven-year-old boys look up to their older brothers. The thing was, I truly believed I could save him. But I couldn't. In my nine-year-old mind after he died, I felt like I'd broken my promise, and I lived with that for years."

"So you joined the Army for James?" she asked.

"It was all he ever talked about so, yes, I joined the Army for my brother. I couldn't have lived with myself if I hadn't."

"What a beautiful thing to do," Sloane said. "I wish I'd known."

"How do you tell someone you're going to war as a means of atoning for something you promised when you were little more than a baby?"

Carter sniffed again.

"My parents were both gone by the time I enlisted, and I suppose the reason I didn't tell anybody why was because my parents' way of coping was to not talk about James, which became my way. We were all so damaged by his death and even though I was young, I think the denials we adopted are what got us through. For me, the denials also helped me cope with my guilt, and while I know it's not the best way to deal with the loss of someone you love so much, I just did what my parents did, and every day it seemed to get easier, and much farther away."

He paused for a moment and looked away.

"I should have told you all that, and I'm sorry I didn't, but I've never talked about James with anybody but you."

Sloane did understand and felt truly sorry for his loss. She felt even worse for his family's need to ignore the loss by not talking more about James. It could have brought them together in a way they'd missed. It could have made them stronger, or closer. That's what had happened when her mother died. She and her dad had kept Mum included as part of them because she was, in every way. And while the loss had been great, it had always been comforting to know her mother through her father's eyes. It had made her dad and her stronger and closer.

"You're lucky to have had him, even if it wasn't for long. I think he would have been proud of you."

"I hope so," he said, taking one more swat at his tears. "Anyway, if you want to catch a sheep, there's one standing in the middle of the path looking at us. I think he might attack, judging from the way he's got his head lowered, and how he's snorting in the dirt. Do they always paw the ground like that when they attack?"

Sloane stood up quickly, but there was nothing ahead. Not a bighorn sheep, not even a tiny little lizard.

"Got ya back for the rattlesnake," Carter said, laughing, and then took hold of her hand and pulled her along the trail.

Yes, *this* was the way they used to be, and Sloane was glad to be back there, if only for a little while.

But could it last? On some level, could they get together again? Or would separate ways be their best course?

CHAPTER SIX

THE HIKE OUT to find the bighorn sheep with Sloane had been fun, Carter reflected as he got on with his afternoon surgery. Much in the way things had used to be between them. Spontaneous. Connecting with each other the way they'd used to connect.

The one thing Carter regretted was that they had only had a couple of hours, as he'd been called back to attend a patient with a sprained wrist. But at least they'd found a small herd of sheep, and Sloane had gotten her pictures. He'd enjoyed seeing her happy, even though her happiness didn't offset the problem that she was such a huge reminder of so many things in his life that had gone bad. He wasn't blaming her for anything. But simply seeing her…

"Mrs. O'Brien?" he asked the older woman who opened her hotel door to the length of its chain and peeked out. She was staying at Cliff Edge, a charming hotel just a few miles away from Red Rock. It accommodated the less active vacationer, which he guessed would be Mrs. O'Brien since he had distinctly heard the clack of an aluminum walker coming from inside her room.

"Are you the doctor? she asked.

"I certainly am. My name's Carter. Carter Holmes."

"Well, Carter Holmes. It's about time you got here. I called over an hour ago."

There was no point in telling her he'd been out hiking and had to practically run the two miles to get back as quickly as he had. Or that he was half-way to being dehydrated, and his back was starting to bother him again, not to mention some very out-of-condition legs that were cramping. When people needed a doctor, they needed a doctor, and nothing else mattered. In a way, he liked the unplanned nature of that. In his surgical practice, nothing had been unplanned. Here, almost everything was, and Carter was finding the challenge of not knowing what he'd be doing in an hour invigorating.

"Sorry to keep you waiting. Next time I'll try to be a little more prompt. Anyway, tell me about your wrist. What happened?"

"I hurt it getting in the shower."

"How long ago?"

"Last night, about this time."

And she'd waited twenty-four hours to call him, which had ruined the evening plans he'd hoped to have with Sloane. Such was the life of a GP, he supposed. And, something he was going to have to get used to.

"Well, why don't you go sit in the chair next to the bed, then I'll take a look."

"Could it be broken, do you think?"

It wasn't likely, considering the way she was using it.

"I should know in a few minutes, after I listen to your heart and lungs, and take your blood pressure."

"All that for a broken wrist?"

"Just being cautious."

Carter watched her walk to the other side of the room and take her seat. She was remarkably sprightly for someone on a walker, and he wondered if she really needed it. But, that was a decision for her real doctor, not him.

"I don't have to get undressed?" Mrs O'Brien asked.

"Nope. But if you could let me listen for a minute..."

Which she did. And for someone her age, which he guessed to be near eighty, she seemed in great shape.

"Everything's normal," he said, taking a gentle hold of the wrist she held out to him. There was no bruising, no swelling, no outcry of pain when he ranged it. "

"Your wrist seems fine to me," he said, finally. "So, when does it hurt."

"It doesn't, but like you said, I'm just being cautious."

And lonely, he guessed. Like him, she was probably all alone in the world, and simply craving a little attention, if even from a stranger. Carter understood that. These last months had been lonely for him, as well.

"I think as a precaution, I'll put an elastic bandage on your wrist, then check back with you every day for a while, to make sure it's getting better."

It hadn't been a necessary medical call, and the bandage wasn't necessary, either. But a few minutes of time might work wonders for her. It had for Carter, when he finally found The Recovery Project.

"Will I be restricted from any activities?" she asked.

"Just rock climbing and canyon hiking," he teased. Instantly, her fixed scowl turned into a pleasant smile. "And no motorcycles."

"I gave those up when I was seventy," Mrs O'Brien said. "My husband and I used to travel cross country on our bikes. The best trip ever was from Seattle, up the coastal highway to Alaska. It was so beautiful, we stayed there a couple of years."

What she'd done in her life wasn't too unlike the

plans he and Sloane had made. In a way, he envied Mrs. O'Brien. She had lived a great life despite her hardships.

"Is that why you're here?" he asked. "Was this someplace you and your husband lived?"

"No, we didn't live here. But we sure did climb every rock and explored every canyon you could find. I wish I was still up to some of it."

"Well, give that wrist a couple of days and maybe we can take a short hike together. I'll see if there are any easy trails around here you could manage."

Mrs. O'Brien beamed from ear to ear. "I'd like that," she said.

And this was the real reason Carter was making this house call—to doctor in a way that was different than he ever had. Or had ever even imagined. It would give him a chance to be personable with his patients, something he'd never done much of before, but Sloane had done all the time. Of course, she would see that as progress. But only if he told her, which he wasn't going to do as he had made the decision he had to start separating from Sloane again. If he didn't start now, he might never get around to it. He had to do it, though. A baby step. The first of many which were all destined to be difficult if every one of them led away from Sloane. But in order to save her, that had to be his course, painful or not.

"I'd say he's good to go." Carter smiled at the couple in front of him.

Mr. and Mrs. Mallory were on holiday with their son, Kevin, who had cystic fibrosis. Clearly not wanting him to miss out on anything, they'd come to ask Carter's opinion on whether Kevin could go on a donkey ride through the canyon. And, while Kevin didn't remind Carter of

James, he brought memories of his brother flooding back, holding on strong.

"You'll have to use caution, of course, and take along the proper equipment, but I'd say Kevin is certainly strong enough to take a donkey ride down into the canyon."

Something his own brother would have loved doing.

"Can you go with us, Doctor?" Judy Mallory asked.

She was nervous. It showed. And Carter understood that better than most. There'd been too many times when he'd gone off to do something with James—something James hadn't always been up to. Playing at the playground. Taking long hikes—long in a child's vision. Going to a friend's house to play video games.

He'd never truly seen his brother as disabled. Of course he'd been so young back then. But his parents had always been cautious, and Carter had always seen that as them depriving James of a real life.

As a child, it had never occurred to him that their restrictions were protective. But here was a boy, not much older than James when he'd died, and his parents wanted him to experience life. They wanted him to be involved in everything he was able to—including a donkey ride down into one of the canyons.

Carter would go along to ease the Mallorys' peace of mind for James' sake. For his brother who'd been restricted from everything.

'What time would you be leaving?" Carter asked.

"We're not sure which day the hotel will arrange it for yet, but it will be late in the day, when it's a little cooler. We're making special arrangements for it to work into Kevin's schedule. You know—between breathing treatments, chest physiotherapy..."

"Well, I've got my hiking boots sitting by the door in

my hotel room, just waiting to go. So, let me know when you're going after you find out and I'll be ready. Barring medical emergencies, of course."

He tousled Kevin's curly hair. The boy wasn't frail the way James had been, and he certainly wasn't plagued by a typical CF cough. As of now his lungs were clear—a condition he'd check again just before their hike. And if ever a smile spoke a thousand words, Kevin's did.

"So, this is what you want to do?" Carter asked the boy as he packed up his medical bag.

"That's why we came here," Kevin said.

"Well, make sure you get plenty of rest, and keep up with your treatments. And if you're doing as well as you're doing right now, whenever the hotel sets the schedule, we're going to have an adventure."

That was what James had always called their excursions—adventures. Because, for him, anything outside their home was an adventure. It did ache, though, knowing how much James would have enjoyed the adventure Kevin was about to have.

Carter nodded to the Mallory family as he exited the room.

Downstairs, in the lobby, he dropped down onto one of the several plush sofas in the sitting area, trying to steady his breathing. He hadn't really exerted himself, and nothing about this felt like the anxiety. This wasn't a panic attack. It had nothing to do with PTSD and everything to do with how crazy bad he still missed his brother. It had been over twenty-six years now, and the pain of it was still acute.

"You OK?" Sloane whispered, sitting down next to him and taking hold of his hand.

"Yes, as far as my PTSD is concerned and no, because I just came from seeing a young boy with CF. It brought back some memories," Carter said, not sure why she was there, but glad she was. "I didn't expect to see you."

"I was just coming back from the spa. I decided to indulge myself a little bit. They have a nice facility here. Maybe you should think about indulging yourself from time to time because you look a little tired. A nice freshen-up might do the trick."

"Have you ever known me to be the spa type?" he asked, giving her a weak smile. "The massages you gave me were everything I ever needed, but to have a stranger do it?"

He faked a shudder.

"All I'm saying is, you need to take better care of yourself. Something seems off."

"I'm just struggling with the pace here. Being on call twenty-four seven has got my system out of whack, but eventually I'll adjust."

"When was the last time you ate, Carter?" she asked in all seriousness.

"Are you trying to diagnosis something?" he snapped. "Because I don't need you doctoring me."

"I'm not trying to doctor you, Carter. I'm just trying to be your friend."

He gave her a curious look for a moment, then stood.

"Then if you're a friend who's concerned about my eating habits, ask me to dinner."

"Really?"

"Everybody's got to eat sometime, I suppose."

"Meaning you haven't been?"

"Meaning I'm waiting for my invitation."

And, to be honest, he couldn't remember his last meal. He hadn't been particularly hungry these past few days—probably due to a combination of new job, new life and Sloane—and if his belly wasn't prompting him to fill it up, he didn't think about food. At least, he hadn't for a day or so.

"Well then, you pick the place and I'll pick up the tab. How does that sound?"

"It sounds like you just made yourself a dinner date."

What if he was getting a little too cozy with Sloane? They did have history. And they both knew that the end of her stay, she'd be leaving while he'd be staying. So, where was the harm in spending a little time together? At the end of it all, Sloane would have the closure she needed, and deserved, and he would simply feel better that he'd done it the proper way this time.

"If you don't mind going to a roadhouse?"

"As in?"

"Lots of noise, probably some dancing, food coming in second to the atmosphere."

It wasn't her kind of place, but it was impersonal, and that's what they both needed. What they didn't need was something intimate like they'd always been drawn to in the past.

"Works for me," she said.

"How about I pick you up around seven?"

"On your bike?"

"Only wheels I've got."

Which meant sitting so close together he'd practically be in between her legs, while her arms were wrapped around his waist. Pleasant thought, but precarious.

"I'll stop by Matt's and grab a helmet for you."

"Then I'll be waiting," she said, pushing herself off the sofa.

Before she walked away, she took a long, hard look at him.

"Are you sure you're good with this? Because I didn't come here to take up all your time, and it seems that's what I'm doing. Especially considering that, well—we're not getting back together."

Carter stood up as well.

"But we can still be friends, can't we?"

Famous last words of most break ups. Words that never came true. Would that be the case with them? Would they say their goodbyes this time, make their promises to remain friends, yet never quite get around to it? Carter hoped not, but he wasn't optimistic. He and Sloane had different lives now. His was just starting while she was well-established in hers, and he didn't see any situation where they could simply meet in the middle and truly be friends. There was too much water under that very old, very shaky bridge now. And, Sloane needed to be away from him.

"Ah, yes. This is where they make the promise then never fulfill it. Is that who we are now, Carter? Two people going through the right motions but who realize those motions aren't going in the same direction anymore?"

"I hope not, but…maybe."

"Well, at least we're being honest. That's progress, I suppose." Sloane pulled out her phone and glanced at the time. "Look, it's getting late and I still need to return a call to one of my surgical patients back home. Then check in with my dad to let him know I haven't dropped off the face of the earth. How about I meet you in the parking lot at six-thirty?"

"Sounds good," he said, just as his phone started to ring.

It turned out to be Mrs. O'Brien who was worried that he'd wrapped her wrist too tightly, and could he stop by to look at it? After he agreed, and hung up, he smiled at Sloane.

"This is really awkward, isn't it?"

"A little bit," she agreed, then walked over and brushed a kiss to his cheek. "See you later."

Later was going to be so, so tough. But facing up to what he'd been was part of his recovery. And if anybody knew what he'd been, it was Sloane. Yet, she still wanted to go out to dinner with him. It wasn't enough to make him optimistic, but it also didn't leave him discouraged as so many of their attempts to be together in the past year had. So, this was good. Yes, very, very good. In fact, it was good enough that if he were a whistling man, he'd leave this hotel, whistling.

Carter lagged back a few steps as they headed toward the motorcycle. She knew why he did that. He liked watching her walk—she'd known that from the first time she'd met him. They'd been walking down the hospital hall and he'd hung back just a step or two, got himself so wrapped up in what he was watching he totally forgot what they'd been talking about. She'd known what was happening. Had felt flattered then, as she still did now.

"Enjoying the view?" she asked.

"Always have," he said. "That part of me hasn't changed."

Sloane stopped and spun around to face him. Smiling.

"I meant the desert. It's vibrant this evening, with all its rusts and golds."

"So did I," he said, trying to act innocent.

"I'll bet you did." Sloane picked up her pace across the parking lot until she reached Carter's motorcycle. "Well, here we are."

"Make sure when you get on the bike your helmet is strapped properly, and your face shield is down."

"Like I didn't always do that?"

"Like you didn't always do it properly."

He checked the way she'd put the helmet on, then

ran his fingers between the chin strap and her quivering flash, causing her to suck in a deep breath.

"Too tight?" he asked.

Sloane shook her head, because right now she knew her words would come out shaking as hard as her hands were. It had been a long, long time since "the Carter effect," as she'd once called it, had been so strong. Way back, during the early days, she'd always quivered when he touched her. But that had worn off after he'd returned home from Afghanistan, and so often his touch had seemed rough and impersonal. But now—this was the old Carter, and her responses where the same as she'd always had with him.

"No, it's good," Sloane finally managed. "Just not sure I like having all this weight on my head."

It was a lie, of course. But he didn't need to know what was really happening to her. Not when he was checking her helmet, not when he was helping her onto the back of his bike, and not when she was practically wrapping herself around him.

All of it caused her to quiver, but that was her secret to keep. Time was, though, when she'd have told him what his touch did to her, when all their plans would be tossed aside and the remainder of the day or night would bring her more than simple quivers.

"It's OK if I lean into you?" Sloane asked him as he engaged the motor and started pushing them forward with his feet.

"Lean, squeeze, grasp—whatever makes you feel safe."

All of it, she thought. It all made her feel not only safe, but incredibly aroused, and as he geared up his motorcycle for the fifteen-mile ride she only hoped it would be a fast fifteen miles. Because those old feelings were coming at her with a vengeance now, and she needed physical distance between them.

Except nothing on the back of his bike gave her that distance, and as they roared off into the sunset she was mentally kicking herself. So far, being around Carter had been almost easy. Nothing about this even came close to *easy*. In fact, in so many ways, being this close to him was one of the toughest things she'd done in a long, long time.

The roadhouse was busy, and people were standing shoulder-to-shoulder in some areas. Mainly near the bar. Carter's first inclination was to squeeze in with them and order a couple of beers, but he caught himself before he took that first step, surprised and yet glad he'd actually remembered he didn't drink.

Sometimes it eluded him, and he came so close. Tonight, though, maybe his self-induced prohibition was to prove himself to Sloane. He wanted to because there was still a wariness about her. It was like she wanted to trust him again, but couldn't quite make it all the way there.

"There's a booth in the back," he shouted over the noise of the crowd. "How about you go get it while I go order us—what? You don't like pizza."

"Why don't you order yourself a pizza and get me some kind of salad?"

"Ranch dressing?" he asked.

"Some things *do* change. I'm liking balsamic vinaigrette now. Or something similar."

He gave her an appreciative nod before he headed to the bar to place his order. Sure, he could have waited for a server to come to the booth, but the noise level in here was too much, and being with Sloane was almost as bad.

But he could deal with it. At least, he hoped he could

because he wanted Sloane to see how far he'd come. Noises could be a trigger, though, so he was keeping his fingers crossed. Very nervous fingers at the moment…

"Iced tea always goes with a salad," he said, setting the glass down in front of Sloane and deliberately climbing into the other side of the booth, as far away from her as he could get.

It wasn't that he didn't like sitting next to her, because he did. He loved it. But not right now, when the noise level was poking at him.

"You remembered," she said, smiling.

"It's what you always ordered," Carter said, setting a plate of lemons in front of her, as well as several packets of sweeteners.

"I remember all your habits," he said, clenching his fists under the table as the noise seemed to keep getting louder and louder. "Left shoe first, then right. A brand new toothbrush every other week. Ice cream every Sunday—strawberry. Never covering your feet under the blankets when you came to bed. Parking in the spot farthest from the hospital and walking the rest of the way, even in the rain."

He relaxed as the fond memories started to take over.

"You're a creature of habit, Sloane. Iced tea goes with salads, beer with pizza, wine with pasta. Did you know you do that—specify your drink according to your food, and never, ever change what goes with what?"

"No," she admitted. "And I didn't know you always watched me so closely. I mean, maybe I can understand why you liked watching me walk away, but my toothbrush habit?"

"Same brand and color of toothbrush every time. And yes, I did watch you closely because it was fun getting to know all the aspects of you."

And she had been glorious to watch as well, especially in those intimate moments when they had come together to dance, or make love, or simply lie on a blanket and gaze at the stars.

"Toothbrush and all my other habits aside, could we move to a quieter booth in the back room? I'm having trouble hearing you."

Was she really having trouble hearing? Or, was she noticing his building anxiety and trying to get him away from the cause of it without being too obvious? Because, if that was the case, it was a kind gesture, and it reminded him of all the times she'd tried to help him, but he'd taken it the wrong way. There were so many things he'd gotten wrong. Things that had caused him to lash out at her when she didn't deserve it. He hadn't seen it then, and he was only just beginning to see it now.

"If we move, will you dance with me?" he asked, then held out a hand to help her out of the booth.

"I'd love to," she said, "as long as it's a slow dance."

They walked hand in hand to the back room but instead of heading to the farthest booth, they fell naturally into the sway of the gentle saxophone playing a solo tune, from the dimly-lit stage, that was meant to seduce. It was a constraining sound, yet a lonely one that told him to hold her tight, to not let go. To dance like it was the last dance of his life. And maybe it was, because without Sloane in his arms, there was no reason to dance.

"You OK?" Sloane whispered into his ear.

"Trying to be," he said, as his hands slid naturally to that familiar spot on her lower back, the place he'd always held her when she raised her arms to twine around his neck.

But she wasn't doing that tonight. Her arms were properly placed on his shoulders in a loose grip, and it made him sad that they'd lost this particular intimacy. And all he could think was that he simply didn't want to be here. Not like this. Not when the memories were too strong, too painful. "Look, could we change our order to a take-away and get out of here?"

"You don't want to dance?" she asked him. "Because we can sit it out, if that's what you'd rather do."

"I um—I just need to leave."

And now, the anxiety was overtaking him again and he knew this time it wasn't going away. Too many memories, too much noise…

"Remember that night we went dancing in the sand?" she asked him.

He stepped away from her. Broke the contact hoping to break the pattern of his attacks. But it wasn't working. Everything was fighting him. Worst of all, he was fighting himself, and losing.

"Sand fleas," he said, attempting to lighten up the moment. But, even to his ears it came out sounding grumpy.

"What?"

"I remember we got pretty chewed up by sand fleas. You were screaming for me to get them off you, when I was trying to get them off me."

He really just wanted to end this—the conversation, the night. Go back to his room, try to sleep and start again in the morning. But the perplexed look on Sloane's face—he'd put that same expression there before, then walked away. This time he needed to stay and fix it.

"I, um—I'm on the verge of an attack, Sloane," he said.

"That's the first time you've ever told me it was coming on. So, you tell me. What do we do?"

And that was the first time she'd ever asked him to tell her how to help. It was something he should probably discuss with his counselor, but to Carter it seemed like he and Sloane had just taken a big step—together.

"Try to change my focus."

"From what to what?" she asked, taking a step closer to him, then starting to reach out to touch him, but stopping herself before she did.

The soothing music of the saxophone stopped, and, in its place, a loud, piercing guitar took over, with offbeat drums thumping in the background. It was hideous to his ears. It sounded like gunfire—like hell had opened up and released a band of screaming banshees.

"From this place too anyplace else."

He looked around for the green, neon exit sign as his breaths started coming faster. Tried remembering that time in Napa where they'd gone up in a hot air balloon and spent the afternoon floating over vineyards. Miles and miles of grapes. A beautiful sight. Carter closed his eyes to picture them, he and Sloane above the clouds and the vines so tiny below them. Floating…drifting… watching Sloane loving the ride. Refocus, Carter. He told himself. Other thoughts. Nicer thoughts.

But the wail of the obnoxious guitar took all that away from him, and his hands started shaking.

"Let's get out of here," she said, taking his hand.

He heard her words, but they were distorting now. They were coming from Sloane, but they were so far away, and he couldn't get to her.

She gave his hand a squeeze and started pulling toward the door.

"Let's go outside, then try to sort this."

He looked at her, not sure whether to pull away and run in the opposite direction to spare her yet another one of his breakdowns or let her help him. He'd never allowed that before, but…

Someone on the dance floor bumped him from behind and Carter drew in a sharp breath, then spun around to confront his attacker. But Sloane stopped him. Physically put herself between the oblivious man who was so wound up with his lady he probably didn't even know there was another person in the room.

"Carter," Sloane said, gently placing both hands on his chest and pushing him back. "Let's go sort this. Now. It's your crisis. You have to guide me through it."

This was a different Sloane altogether. She'd never reacted to his attacks this way before. In the past, she'd always been too sympathetic, too bending. But not this time.

"Sure," he said, following her as they made their way off the crowded dance floor and headed straight for the rear exit.

Once they were out, Carter fell to the ground, and simply lay there, looking up at the stars, still gasping, still struggling to fight his way through this. Then, when Sloane joined him there on the ground, she simply sat with him in the shadow of a smelly trash bin and held his hand. For now, that's all he wanted.

CHAPTER SEVEN

OPENING THE HOTEL room door, her mind still on Carter all these hours later, Sloane headed directly into the hall and nearly tripped over him. He was sitting on the floor outside her door, eyes closed but not asleep.

"Since I dropped you off at your hotel, I assumed you'd still be there, sound asleep," she said.

Or pacing the floor for hours, which was something he'd used to do. Last night, however, when she'd suggested they call her hotel to send a car, and then subsequently dropped him off at his room, he'd been quiet. Subdued. She hadn't expected that. Hadn't expected him to acquiesce so easily. But he had. He'd simply kissed her on the cheek and walked away from the hotel as if he *hadn't* just been on the verge of what had looked as if it might be a major meltdown.

So...was this program Carter was on working for him? Getting counseling...training bears. Sloane hadn't been sure about it when he'd told her, but she was seeing something different now. Something more like the man she'd used to know. And while it excited her, it also scared her. because she wondered how long this effect would last before he'd revert. Or *would* he revert?

Maybe. Maybe not. For Carter's sake, she hoped he wouldn't.

"Been there long?" she asked, and her heartbeat went a little crazy, the way it always did the first instant she saw him.

"A couple of hours."

"Without knocking?"

"Didn't want to disturb you." He picked up a bag from the floor and handed it to her. "Apple, banana, salad, cookies—"

"I don't eat cookies," Sloane interrupted.

"I do," he said, finally standing. "I'm sorry about what happened tonight. Normally I can feel these things coming on, and I use the grounding techniques I've learned when I don't feel like I can simply walk away. Or in some cases run away."

"What grounding techniques?" she asked, holding out her hand to him to help him off the floor.

"Sound—turning on loud music, but not like what we were hearing last night. Classical works for me, especially a rousing Beethoven symphony. Normally his seventh does the trick. I know it by heart and I hum along, which gets me away from my anxiety."

He smiled.

"Especially if I conduct it."

"You've learned to conduct?"

Carter laughed.

"Hell, no. But swinging my arms around pretending that's what I'm doing takes me to a different place, which is where I need to be."

"If you want, I could teach you to conduct."

Sloane had an undergrad degree in music and for a while had thought about becoming a professional. But the lure of healing changed all that.

"Or I could just do it my way," he said, not intending to

sound contentious. “Because I like the freedom of doing it my way. It’s cathartic and energizing, and it works.”

“I didn’t mean to—”

There she was, trying to take over when he clearly needed to guide his own journey. To help Carter, she was going to have to be more aware of her own actions.

“That’s OK.”

“You know this isn’t easy for me,” she said.

Walking away from him in less than two weeks wasn’t going to be easy, either. But he wasn’t offering her any hope for a future together, and she was trying hard not to get her hopes up.

“Me either,” he said. “Which is why if the music doesn’t work—and sometimes it doesn’t—there are various smells that will snap me back. A lot of people are triggered by smell, and for me peppermint oil works, so I always carry a vial of it.”

From his pocket he produced a small silver vial, usually used for carrying nitroglycerin pills, and held it out to her.

Sloane took it, uncapped it, and immediately smelled the scent. It was amazing watching him take charge of his PTSD episodes. She hadn’t seen this before and she was so—proud. Yes, proud of him.

“I’m so glad it’s working for you.”

“Most of the time it does. Sometimes, though…”

Carter lowered his voice as a group of tourists walked by them. “Sometimes it doesn’t, and the problem is I don’t know when it will or won’t work. Sometimes the PTSD wins no matter what I do.”

“And last night?”

“A little bit of win, and a little bit of being defeated.”

“Does that happen often?” Sloane asked. Because

from what she had seen, he'd been able to control his attack much more than he hadn't been able to control.

"More than I'd like it to. But overall my number of episodes has decreased. If I feel something coming on, half the time I can—I don't call it control so much as divert or distract it. That was a huge emphasis in the first part of my program—taking charge of yourself when it's trying to take over. It's not easy, and sometimes it's so damn difficult it drops you to your knees then causes you to curl up in a ball and cry. But when you succeed—it's a feeling I can't describe."

The thought of Carter curled into a ball broke her heart, and she was the one who wanted to cry. But the focus here was him, and she had to remember that. To turn this into anything about her could defeat him.

"And when you don't succeed?"

It used to be he'd take it out on her. Screaming. Throwing things. She'd put away all her breakables months ago.

"It's a toss-up. Sometimes if I fight myself hard enough I can change the direction of my episode. Or lessen the blow of it. Sometimes, though, it's easier to simply go someplace else. Get away from people. Even hide, if I have to. But my counselor will be helping me make some changes with all that when I get back to the program."

It sounded good, and Sloane felt encouraged for him. Especially as he was beginning to take responsibility for his actions whenever he could. The old Carter had been so full of blame. It had been directed at anyone who happened to be near him when he broke down.

Yet last night—none of that had happened. The episode had occurred, but he'd beaten it.

"So, why are you here, Carter?" she finally asked. "Sitting on the floor outside my hotel door?"

"Not really sure why. I keep an empty booze bottle next to my bed as a reminder of where I've been, and something about that bottle scared me when I got to my room. If it had been full… Anyway, I called my counselor, as we're supposed to do when we feel ourselves slipping and told her how I wanted to go to the bar and drink. One of the things she told me to do was go take a walk to clear my head. Which is why I ended up here."

"How often are you tempted to drink?" she asked him.

"Every time I have a meltdown. Which is why we're required to call one of our counselors. It becomes a major step in the prevention of something we're not supposed to do. In my case, drink. If we don't, and we do give in, then we start back at the beginning of the program, if they even allow us back in."

"Isn't that kind of harsh?"

"PTSD is harsh. You couldn't expect the treatment to be any less harsh. So, I keep the bottle nearby as a remind of what I've lost and what I stand to gain."

"Good for you, Carter," she said, stepping back and motioning him into her room. "So, it's four miles, Carter. You walked four miles to get here? Because you thought I would do—what?"

"I'm not expecting anything from you, Sloane. I just wanted you to see that I can control myself sometimes. That I don't always get pulled under."

"I did see that in the roadhouse, how you went from just on the verge to well, something almost calm. Or, accepting."

"Not accepting. That's giving in. Too many people do that because it's easy. I did that when I left you because fighting the demon is so hard and sometimes it's less painful to simply let it take you over."

"And all those months when I kept telling you to fight…"

"I was fighting you. Because you, in a lot of ways, were the demon—the one who was always there, being my conscience when I didn't have one. The one who was always reminding me that once upon a time I had been a good enough person to win someone like you, but all that had changed. I wasn't good anymore. Didn't deserve anything or anyone."

"You should have told me," Sloane said as the door closed behind her and she realized just how small her room was with both of them in there.

While she, herself, wasn't given to panic attacks, she could sympathize with Carter with one aspect of his—claustrophobia. She was certainly feeling it right now. Cramped space. Not enough air. His scent was the same—the aftershave she'd given him years ago, that he'd never quit using. And so much of the man she'd used to love was showing through right now.

"There was nothing to tell, because I didn't know. A lot of the time, I'm figuring it out as I go."

"And all this new self-awareness—do you trust it?"

Sloane wanted to. But she wasn't quite ready for that. Not yet. It wasn't as if she wanted to make him prove himself. It was just that she'd tried so hard and been so hurt. Now she was just plain afraid to hope, to trust, to give herself over to something that might or might not happen. It was too much to deal with—especially since she'd thought she was at a place in her life where she could take a step or two forward. That was until she saw Carter again. Now, she was confused. And, conflicted. There were too many emotions, too many memories running through her to deal with. Especially not here, alone in a hotel room with Carter.

"Sometimes I almost do." He sighed heavily. "But I don't let myself get too heavily invested in it because what if I fail again? I've already hit the bottom once, and if I do it again I won't bounce back. Not that I'm bouncing now. But at least I can see the changes I need to make, and I understand what I've got to cope with for the rest of my life better than I used to."

He walked up to Sloane and stopped just short of pulling her into his arms. But he did reach out and brush his fingers over her cheek.

"I'm sorry for what I did to us, Sloane. I could see it happening—see what I was doing to you—but I couldn't stop it. You were the only one who was really there, and even though I knew that I couldn't control myself. You were an easy target because you loved me."

Sloane reached up to Carter's face and took hold of his hand. The feel of him was so good. She'd missed it—missed the simple things. The touching, the looks they'd exchange that said so much, the smiles. But she couldn't let herself fall into the trap of believing in him again. He'd hurt her so badly, so often. And believing in him—that was *her* demon to fight. Because every ounce of her wanted to. But every ounce of her knew that loving Carter made her too vulnerable.

"I did love you. Maybe I even still do, in some ways. But you hurt me so badly, and while I know it wasn't your fault I can't do that again. Can't go back to that place or to who we were. That doesn't exist anymore."

"It wasn't my intention to hurt you," Carter said, stepping away from her. "And it was never my intention to see that look of confusion, or maybe even apprehension, that was on your face a couple minutes ago, when you found yourself alone in the same hotel room as me."

He crossed over to the far wall and sat down on the arm of an easy chair.

"Remember that first time we went away together for a weekend? Palm Beach?"

Sloane did, but she didn't want to.

"The room was so tiny we had to crawl over the bed to get from one side to the other."

But it hadn't mattered, because even though they'd practically been on the beach, they hadn't left the room except to eat. It had been a horrible place to stay, but her memories were nothing but good.

"That was back when we were young and naïve."

It seemed like so long ago, and so much had happened since then.

"Whatever happened to those two people?" he asked, twisting on the chair, trying to favor his lower back, obviously looking for a more comfortable position. "They were a pretty good couple, weren't they?"

"The best," she whispered, promising herself she wouldn't cry. "Young love like that is always the best."

So many hopes, so many dreams. Now look at them. Barely able to look at each other, let alone speak. This wasn't the way her dream was supposed to have turned out. She'd had it since she was a little girl—to find her one true love, settle down together, live happily-ever-after.

There was nothing happy in the way she lived now. There was no one true love.

"Well, we were good at it."

She nodded.

"Very good at it."

Sloane leaned back against the window and stared at him for a moment and her breath caught. This was Carter she was talking to now—not some difficult manifestation of him. If only she could hold on to that—to him—and not let him get away.

"Carter, when you left me…did you hate me? I never knew. You said I was one of your demons, and I actually do understand that. But did you—or maybe *do* you—hate me? You were so distant for so long, and everything I tried to do—it always just made you angry. I did try," Sloane said as the tears finally came. "It wasn't easy standing back, watching you self-destruct, but it got to the point where there wasn't anything else I could do. I'd tried everything, and the harder I tried the more you resisted me—I'm beginning to realize why, which makes me wonder if you hated me."

"I didn't hate you," he said, taking several steps in her direction, then stopping. "Not then—not now. But I couldn't live with you. Not anymore."

"Why?" she asked.

"Maybe because I couldn't live with myself. There were always too many reminders of someone I was never going to be again. Everywhere I looked."

Sloane swiped away a tear as he crossed the room and pulled her into his arms. It felt good being there. But it didn't feel like she belonged. There was nothing natural here. Nothing from before.

Still, Carter's arms were strong, and right now she needed strong arms. Needed someone to lean on—someone who understood why, in this moment, she wasn't the same person she'd been either.

Resting her head against his chest, she listened to the steady, strong beat of his heart and recalled when that heart had been weakened by his injuries, and his chart had listed him as "critical." He'd always reached for her when he was awake, and she had always been there for him to hold, believing he'd needed her strength for recovery.

That was what she'd wanted to do, anyway. To lend her strength, her support, everything she was, to help make him whole. But that had never happened, because Carter had never healed.

"What else could I have done, Carter?" Sloane asked, her head still on his chest.

They stood in silence for a moment, she still in his embrace, he still holding her tightly against him. No kisses, no caresses. Simply memories of this same embrace, so many times over the years. She'd come to count on it, to love it, to respond to it in a way she knew she would never respond to the embrace of another man. It was still a proper embrace, one meant for support, but the line was hers to draw. Or step across.

"It was never you," he whispered, tilting her face up to his. "I tried, Sloane. God knows, I tried. But I couldn't make it work. Every time I looked at you—every time we were together…"

Sloane reached up, put her fingers over his lips to silence him. This wasn't what she'd had in mind when she'd thought of closure, but maybe she'd been wrong about that all along. Maybe she'd been too analytical about him, too much his nurse and not his lover.

She reached for him, placing her shaking hand on the back of his neck, lifting her lips to his. "This is what's left," she whispered. "Only this."

It was a bittersweet reminder of why she was there. But she wanted this. Wanted a different memory of their parting. And there was no shame in her for what she wanted, as she'd expected there might be. This man had been a large part of her life for so long—she deserved to have what she wanted.

They kissed—first lightly, but then their desperation grew quickly. His tongue was in her mouth, searching places it had searched a thousand times before, and her hips were tilting so naturally to his, her back arching to the touch of his hand as it always had done.

Her body was sending a message, and she could feel his answer, even though words were not spoken. They didn't have to be. His eyes said yes. But there was some doubt in them. In his, probably in hers, too.

His tongue sought hers again, and this time he ran his hands through her wild red hair, separating the strands with his fingers. She loved the way he did that—so delicately, yet so provocatively. It always caused her flesh to quiver, always caused her breath to shorten. He pulled her even closer to him, until nothing separated them but fabric. It was as if he wanted to fold her inside him, keep her safe the way he'd always kept her safe.

Pushing away from him just slightly, Sloane pressed the palm of her hand against his chest and pushed him backwards onto the bed. Then she tumbled down on top of him, interlocking their hands above his head. At first she nibbled his chin, then moved lower, to his throat, where she pressed light kisses.

Removing one of her hands from his, she raised herself up just slightly and ran her fingertips over his face. He'd used to be clean-shaven. His face was as smooth as a baby's bottom, she'd always teased him. But she liked the feel of his stubble. It was a new look for him—slightly rough, definitely sexier than anything she'd ever seen on him.

"You feel so good," she finally whispered.

"Is this what you want, Sloane?" he asked. "Because we either stop right here, or..."

It was what *he* wanted—what he'd always wanted. Only with Sloane.

There'd been other women these past few months—women he'd met along the way. They'd wanted him—he'd wanted them. But somehow something had always stopped him, made the moment go bad or go away.

It was Sloane, he realized, now that he had her back in his arms again, and her lush curves and her soft skin were everything he remembered. No one was Sloane. No one could be Sloane. Not ever.

Which was why this between them now was *not* a good idea. One time, maybe two times, and then she'd be out of his life—but this time forever. That was the only way it could end. He'd walk away again, only this time he'd set her free before he did.

His last memories of them together like this were so bad. He'd been selfish, his words hateful. Which was what he needed to remember. The look on her face then—there'd been so much pain, so much confusion. The way she was looking at him now was a different look—more knowing, more mature. But it was still Sloane. And he had no right to her.

Still, when he felt her slide over in bed he didn't stop her. Nor did he stop her when she unfastened his jeans, then eased them along with his briefs down over his hips.

Carter sighed again when she raised up slightly and removed his pants all the way. Her exploration took her places only Sloane knew.

He shut his eyes, thinking about how unbelievably good this felt, physically and emotionally, and when Sloane gave a throaty moan then slid her mouth from his chest, then on down.

"Look at me," she said finally, disengaging from him for a moment and urging him into bed.

He did, and he saw that her eyes were fully open, locked on his eyes. Searching for something? he thought. Probably something he didn't have.

"What?" he asked.

"Just look," she said, positioning herself face to face with him again. They were so close they were breathing the same air. "So I can look at you."

That was when Carter knew what this was about. It was about taking all the ugliness he'd brought down on them and turning it into something good and beautiful, so she could walk away from him for the last time. It was what Sloane needed.

"You've always been so beautiful," he said as he reached across and began to ease her shirt up over her head. She helped with her bra, and they both worked together to remove all the clothes that stood between them.

But they didn't hurry. They lingered over caresses and kisses, each remembering what the other liked, each trying to give pleasure. It was a fragile experience, slow and familiar, yet eventually developing into something with a new, different urgency—like the one they'd known at the beginning, which had eventually slipped away into a more intimate proficiency over time.

He took his time, nuzzling against her, knowing he would not be here again. He was nibbling and kissing his way up to her earlobe, where she'd always been ticklish, and understanding he would never again hear her whispered laugh again his cheek. He could feel her thigh muscles harden as he slid his hand down her belly, occasionally stopping to kiss the trace he was making. She quivered when he did that—when he kissed her belly, her hip, moved around to her bottom. He was taking much the same trail she had when she'd kissed him, only without the scars.

"Ooh..." Sloane whispered as he rolled her onto her back and slipped inside her.

This was the way it had been—the way it should have always been. And as he began to find his rhythm he heard a strangled sob. Not from pain, but from heartbreak. He was willing to stop, to pull himself away, but Sloane was not, and she took up his rhythm—a slow snapshot. A memory yet to be made.

After several hard thrusts against him, urging him on with her, there was nothing he could do but give himself over to the exquisite tightness, the heat, the increasing intensity. But first, before he let the rise and fall of impending climax sweep him under, he reached down and stroked her cheek, then her hair.

"I never meant to hurt you," he said.

"I know."

Maybe she did. He hoped so, because Sloane was the only woman he'd ever loved. And that was the closure he wanted her to have—that knowledge.

"Please, Carter," she whispered.

And that was all it took. He could no longer hold back, even though the idea of not continuing was tinged with regret. But as she forced her hips into him, and he pounded harder and harder to meet her urgency, all thoughts of anything but this moment disappeared.

"You feel so good," he whispered, his voice coming in gasps between thrusts. Then came that maddening clutch on him she always took and held, the heat, the voices in his head urging him on...

Suddenly there was only now. And he wanted it all. Hard, fast. No thoughts about anything before and after.

"Sloane!" he cried out as the moment came to its brink.

But she said nothing in return. Nor did she shout out, pant or moan.

Sloane responded to her need with his own until she was exhausted, curling herself against his chest the way she always did afterwards. But this time he felt the moisture of her tears on his arms. So, he held on to her tighter, like it was the last night of the world.

In many ways, it was.

CHAPTER EIGHT

THE DAY STARTED off like any other. Or at least like any other day Sloane had had in the past six or seven months. She woke up alone, with no idea where Carter was, and really no expectation of finding him.

He'd showered, she discovered, and taken his medical bag, so maybe that meant he'd gone off to work. She hoped so because, despite her big mistake last night—and it truly was a huge one—all she wanted this morning was to know that what they'd done hadn't shaken Carter to the very core and set him off in some new direction with his PTSD.

After a quick shower, Sloane pulled on her clothes and walked over to the window, parted the curtains and looked out. What she expected to find she wasn't sure. Certainly not Carter, lounging poolside the way some of the early birds were already doing. despite a little November chill in the air. In fact, unless someone here at the Red Rock was ill, she didn't expect to find him at all.

But that was her habit—always scanning a crowd, looking for him. She'd been doing that since he'd left her, never quite sure what she'd do if she did happen to see him.

A knock on her hotel room door startled her, and she spun around to stare at it for a moment before she crossed the room to open it. She didn't really expect to find Carter standing in the hall either, wanting to come back in, although a tiny part of her did want that. Which meant that tiny part of her was disappointed when the person in the hall turned out to be one of the hotel staff, carrying a tray with food.

"I didn't order that," she said, not yet stepping back to allow him entrance.

"It's from the house doctor. He stopped by the kitchen a couple hours ago and left the order." He pulled back the linen covering on the tray to reveal a bowl of fresh fruit, yogurt and toast. Her favorite breakfast, actually.

"Could you put it on the table next to the bed, please?" she asked, feeling a little embarrassed by the rumpled condition of her bedding.

"Yes, ma'am," he said, sliding in past her, leaving the tray and hurrying out.

In Sloane's mind he'd made note of the state of the bed and was on his way to tell all his co-workers what he'd discovered. In reality she was sure he saw morning-after beds all the time and probably didn't even pay attention to them.

A morning-after bed. Her and Carter's morning-after bed.

"What did I do?" Sloane moaned as she slid into her shoes, deciding to forego the breakfast in favor of going to find Carter, so she could tell him that last night had been a one and only.

She texted him on her way out the door, asking him if they could talk. Surprisingly, he texted back immediately, telling her he was with a patient at another hotel, then had two more appointments before he went to his office. What he offered her was some time after work, although he didn't know when that would be. Oddly enough, he ended his text with, Hands off this time, Soane. I can't go through that again.

The message hurt in so many ways—because that was basically what he'd said months ago, when he'd moved out of their bedroom. Still, it was the message she would have texted him if he hadn't beaten her to it. Because, like Carter, she couldn't go through it again either.

She'd missed that part of their life as she'd missed so many other parts and getting involved the way they had last night didn't fix things. Didn't even come close to helping either.

They were adults, though, repeating a doomed past, and that was all it was. A moment of weakness destined to fail. She laughed bitterly. A moment that had never failed to be good. Now, wasn't *that* just ironic? The one place where they could come together perfectly turned out to be the one place they had no business being.

Well, that wasn't the cheeriest of thoughts, but it was the one she took with her when she left the hotel, not sure what she was going to do with her day—especially since this wasn't the vacation she'd planned. Or wanted. But maybe, deep down, it was. Maybe she'd planned to find a little bit of Carter here, or even Carter himself, and she'd been fooling herself all the time.

Why, after all, would she have even thought of a place like Forgeburn, let alone come here? Because Carter had mentioned it so often?

A text message interrupted her thoughts.

Permissions from the Department of National Resources just came through. Going down into the canyon with Kevin Mallory and family early this evening. Easy hike. Want to come?

Suddenly her prospects for the day looked much brighter.

Sure. When?

Probably around five. I'll let you know more after I check the weather then make sure he's good to go.

Maybe a morning lounging by the pool wasn't a bad idea at all. She had her electronic reader with her, and a queue of romance novels and mysteries she'd been promising herself she'd read. So, a quick change into a pair of gray jersey pants and a pink t-shirt, and her morning was set.

Sure, she would have been better off, and smarter in the long run, if she'd gone out with one of the tour guides. But when had she ever done the smart thing when it came to Carter? Which meant this was merely history repeating itself. Carter called and she ran, with her heart pounding a little harder. And that meant she wasn't over him. Oh, she'd probably already known that somewhere in her muddled thinking. But to admit it?

It was going to turn into a problem, no doubt. Just like last night, while it had been wonderful, was a problem. Because if he wanted a repeat of it she wasn't sure she could say no.

One *come hither* crook of his finger and she'd *gone thither* all over the place. For hours. Some of the time she'd even taken the lead.

It was still a good five hours before he would get the plans underway to take Kevin down into the canyon, which meant free time. He'd thought about asking Sloane if she wanted to have lunch with him. At least that had been his full intention. But when he'd been called to the

Sunrise Canyon Hotel and told his ride would meet him at the Red Rock, there wasn't much else he could do but go. Work was his primary goal here, and as much as he wanted to give Sloane her opportunity to say what he was sure she'd want to say, it hadn't worked out. Not yet. And, maybe a large part of that was his fault, because he didn't want to hear it.

Sure, they were over. They had to be over. But the reality of it wasn't easy because he didn't want to hurt her more than he already had.

"So, how far along is your wife?" Carter asked the man who was driving him in his truck. Like so many people out here, he lived in an isolated area, but Hugh Lewiston had managed to get his wife, Shelly, to the Sunrise Canyon Hotel, which was about ten miles closer to Carter than the Lewiston ranch was.

"She's right on her due date now. It's our first," Hugh said, beaming.

"Has she been seeing a doctor?"

Hugh shook his head. "Once in the early part of her pregnancy. He said she was healthy, so we didn't see any point in spending money for something we already knew."

Carter leaned his head against the back of the truck seat and closed his eyes. "No tests or anything?"

He'd delivered babies in Afghanistan—the babies of civilian women—but always in a hospital. They'd known to come in, known there was medical help for them there. But Shelly Lewiston? This made him nervous.

"How old is Shelly?" he asked, looking over at Hugh and guessing him to be in his mid-forties. Which meant, if Shelly was close to that age, she might be more prone to problems with delivery and also with the baby.

"Just turned forty-two."

"Has she been sick much during her pregnancy?"

"Not once," Hugh said. "In fact she was working the ranch with me up until yesterday. That's when she got a backache and decided it was time to go put her feet up. She wasn't having labor pains, though. Not until this morning."

"And how far apart are they?"

Probably a couple of minutes. I really didn't stay long enough to count much. I thought it was better to call you, then come get you, since the road out there is a little tricky and I didn't want you getting lost."

Carter gritted his teeth as the truck hit a rut, then looked down at his hands…white knuckles balled into fists. But this wasn't PTSD. It was simply a surgeon going into an unknown situation, preparing to do God only knew what.

Suddenly, for the first time since he'd climbed in next to Hugh, he was actually able to relax. And he wanted to call Sloane and tell her. But he didn't. What was the point?

"Well, I'm glad you did. Home births aren't always easy. Or in this case a hotel birth."

"You don't think there are going to be any problems, do you?" Hugh asked as they turned into the parking lot of the Sunrise Canyon Hotel.

There was quite a crowd gathered. Probably two dozen people were standing in the parking lot, making what seemed like a tunnel of people for Carter to pass through to get inside. And when he did he knew why they were out there. Shelly was sprawled out on one of the lobby couches, moaning, while at least six women stood around her, ready to help deliver the baby.

"OK," he said, making his way through the crowd, sounding as confident and in charge as he ever had in his life. "How far apart are her contractions?" he asked of anyone who'd answer.

"Continual," one of the women said.

"Anyone here medical?" he asked as he set his bag down on the floor and immediately took Shelly's pulse. She was too involved in another moan to notice him. "Nurse, doctor, midwife, medic?"

When no one answered a wave of nausea washed through him, but he fought it down and positioned himself to examine Shelly.

"Just relax," he said to her, and he took a look.

Sure enough, the baby was crowning. In fact it was fighting its way out like a football player fighting to get through the line. "You're going to be a mother in just a minute here."

That caused Shelly to look up. "Are you the doctor who was an Army surgeon?" she managed to force out.

"I was," he said, as he snapped on a pair of gloves and went to work. "But I traded all that for this."

"Why?" she asked, as her breathing started turning into more of a panting.

"PTSD. Thought Forgeburn was a good place to work through some of it."

"Sorry to hear that," she said, then raised herself up as a hard contraction hit. "Hope the military is taking care of you."

She addressed it with such a lack of shock or pity it surprised him. One of the things he'd learned in his program was that admitting the problem was the first step. Admit it to yourself, then to other. In other words, it was nothing to be ashamed of, so why bother trying to hide it?

"I'm in a great program." He smiled and, surprisingly, it wasn't forced. This was the first time he'd just come out and admitted it to someone who wasn't either in his program or close to him, like Sloane and Matt. It felt good. Almost like a weight had been lifted from his shoulder. No doubt all of Forgeburn would learn of his condition by the end of the day, but that didn't matter. He was going to be doctor to some of them, and they had the right to know.

"So, are you ready to become a mother because…" He turned the baby's head just slightly. "Next time you feel the urge, give me a big push."

The woman seated behind Shelly prepared to sit her up, and when the next contraction came, in only a few seconds, all the ladies standing around watching yelled, "Push!"

Which was exactly what Shelly did as Hugh staggered over to a chair on the other side of the room and then collapsed into it.

"One more push and—" He glanced over to make sure Hugh was OK, then literally caught the baby as it slid out. "Somebody—in my bag I've got a handheld suction…" He looked at Shelly, who was stretched out flat on the sofa, trying to see her baby. "As soon as I get him cleaned up and examined you can hold your little boy."

"A boy?" Hugh called from across the room as the bystanders who'd stayed in the hall during the blessed event started to cheer.

"A boy…" Shelly whispered, watching Carter clamp the cord, cut it, then put Ilotycin in the baby's eyes to prevent conjunctivitis after the birth.

One of the woman stepped forward to wipe the baby down, then wrapped him in a soft blanket that had come from another hotel guest. During this, Carter checked Shelly to make sure there was no excessive bleeding and that the placenta had been safely delivered.

"Want to hold your son?" he asked, taking the baby

from the woman who was holding the newborn. "Because I think he's waiting for you."

Carter lowered the baby into Shelly's arms, then stepped back as Hugh made his way over to take his first look. Then wobbled on his feet again.

Carter who was on his way up caught Hugh, who was on his way down, and lowered him to the ground, where he knelt beside his wife, then reached out to stroke his crying son's hand.

"He's got a set of lungs on him, doesn't he?"

"Good, strong cry," Carter said, backing away from the scene as he saw Cruz Montoya stroll into the room.

"Somebody call for me?"

"I did," Carter said. "It was an easy birth, but because of the mother's age I'd like to get her to a hospital, or even the clinic over in Whipple Creek—just to have some routine tests run and maybe watch her for a day."

"You're flying with me?" Cruz asked.

"Yep," he said, giving no thought to how nervous he'd been last time he'd flown. One hurdle down and stomped into the ground, Carter thought, as he and Cruz helped mother and child into the old green canvas, war-variety stretcher Cruz brought with him. And that's just what he did, with no qualms. He helped carry the stretcher out, then climbed into the helicopter without so much as a rolling stomach or a bead of sweat.

"I heard you made your PTSD public," Cruz said, as he fastened in for the flight.

Carter chuckled. News really did travel fast in Forgeburn.

"They say it went perfectly, and then Dr. Holmes and Cruz took them over to Whipple Creek Clinic for the night."

"They flew?" Sloane asked the server who'd brought her a fruit juice smoothie.

It was warm for November, and after an hour of lounging she'd finally given in and changed into her swimsuit. The sun on her exposed skin felt good, even though overall she was rather pale. That came from staying inside, working too much. She rarely had leisurely days like this, when she could simply sit and bask.

"I heard the crowd cheered him on as he climbed into the helicopter."

"Why would they do that?" Sloane asked the young man.

"Because they all knew how hard it was for him to do that."

"Then they all know—?"

"The whole PTSD thing? Sure. He talked about it when he was delivering the baby. But it's no big deal. Everybody's got their problems. The doc's aren't any better or worse than anybody else's."

Maybe that was true. At least, in Forgeburn. But Forgeburn wasn't a typical sampling of the real world and, someday, Carter would have to face that without his cheering squad. This was a start, though—and an opportunity to prove himself to the people who needed him. And she was encouraged because he was finding a life here. Maybe not the one she'd expected of him. But a life, nonetheless. He deserved that.

"Any news on how they're doing?"

She wasn't concerned so much about mother and baby because in Carter's hands they would be fine. But she was concerned about Carter.

"Only that the doctor is back in his office and Cruz is taking a small tour group out for some sightseeing."

Should she casually wander over to Carter's office?

Maybe to congratulate him on the delivery? Or to simply see how he was doing? She wanted to. But she also wanted him to come tell her. She had always included him on the big events, and now she wanted him to do the same for her. So, she took a sip of her smoothie, then continued reading her book. It had been a big morning for Carter, and she was glad he'd managed every bit of it on his own. That's what he needed to help him regain all his confidence—independence. It was a double-edged sword, however. For Carter, it was good. But for her…

CHAPTER NINE

CARTER HADN'T SEEN Sloane since the evening before, even though they'd texted a little. But that was fine, because after delivering Shelly and Hugh's baby he'd come back and got busy in the clinic with the usual things. Scrapes and abrasions, broken bones, a couple of open head gashes—nothing serious.

In fact his tiny waiting room had been full of people talking about what they were calling "the miracle birth," even though there had been no miracle involved. Now everyone was gone, and Sloane was on his mind again.

"Look, I'm going to step out for a little while. Call me if someone comes in."

It wasn't as if he needed to see her—especially since she was going out with him and the Mallory family later. But he wanted to see her, and there was a wide difference between wanting and needing. At least that was what he was telling himself as he got on his motorcycle—thoughtfully returned by the roadhouse owner—and headed down the road.

What was he hoping for? He didn't know. But he was hoping for something, and hope was something he hadn't had in a long, long time.

For sure, today had been a lazy one. Between sleeping late, then lounging, followed by an hour in the spa and another hour having a facial, Sloane was about as pampered as she cared to be—because being pampered meant empty thoughts, which meant an open door to thinking about Carter.

She hoped Carter was still up to it, physically, because he had had a challenging physical day, and she worried that he looked so tired every time she'd seen him since coming to Forgeburn. It was probably nothing, she decided. He was simply trying to re-adjust to his new life. Still, she worried. It was too ingrained in her to stop.

"You look tired," Carter said, stepping up behind her as she sat in the café sipping a smoothie.

"Funny. I was just thinking the same thing about you."

"Getting used to the pace, little by level. I worked harder in surgery, standing on my feet for hours, but the whole re-learning process here is taking it out of me. Mind if I sit down."

Sloane nodded, then even offered him a sip of her smoothie—another one of those ingrained things. She always shared with Carter, as he did with her. In fact, some of their better moments involved feeding each other, teasing a meatball to her lips, teasing a bite of bread to his lips. Yes, they'd shared food, and so many other things, so the smoothie offer came naturally. So did his acceptance of it.

"Are you ready for Kevin's big adventure?" she asked. "I saw him on my way in. He's so excited."

"I'm glad we could do this for him. Every little boy deserves a big adventure." Carter reached across, took her cup, and helped himself to another sip.

"So does every big boy," Carter said, sliding the smoothie back to her, then taking hold of her hand when she reached for it. "I'm glad you're going, Sloane. And not just as a doctor, but as the person I've loved having adventures with."

It fit so well there that she was almost taken in by him. Did he want a repeat of what had happened last time he'd come to her hotel room? Did he expect them to get back together?

"What are you doing, Carter?" she asked. "Are you here to see Kevin, or is something else going on?" She pulled back her hand. "Maybe another patient?"

"Just hanging around," he said. "It's still an hour before we go on that hike, and since I had nothing else to do…" He shrugged.

"You had nothing else to do so you thought you'd come to the hotel and do me in your spare time?"

"One time, and see how you are? No hidden motives here, Sloane. I was just hoping to see you."

Sloane laughed.

"Have I always been so…suspicious?"

"I think it's something I probably put there. Another thing to regret, I suppose."

"If you want to spend the rest of your life regretting that's up to you. Personally, I don't, which is one of the reason I came here—to confront my own issues."

"Issues I caused?"

"Some, maybe. But also issues I allowed you to cause."

"I never meant to do that."

"But it's so easy to lash out at the one closest to us, isn't it? I know you never meant to hurt me, and I'm not holding it against you that you did. And that, Carter, is probably the biggest issue I've resolved since I've been here and witnessed how hard you're trying to overcome your own issues. I know that it probably sounds more sentimental than you like, but I'm proud of you."

"Actually, sometimes it's good to hear that. Especially

from the people you respect. Or, in your case, respect the most."

Respect, not love. That was another of his issues, being hurt every time she was forced to come to terms with what Carter wanted from his life, and it was painfully obvious it wasn't her. In time, she would get over it. Or at least, be able to put it away in a place she didn't revisit. But until then, that little twinge of sadness still overtook her from time to time. "Well, the next thing you should hear is that it's time to get started with Kevin's trek into the wilderness. So, have you got all the medical supplies we might need packed?"

"I do. And I've probably overpacked, trying to think of every scenario that could happen."

"He's going to be fine, Carter. His own pulmonary specialist cleared him, you cleared him, and there's really nothing to hold him back. Kevin and his family know the risks—all we have to do is make sure none of those risky situations happen." She reached over and took hold of his hand and said, very tenderly, "This isn't your brother. His condition isn't like your brother's was, and nor are his prevailing health issues. I know it's hard to separate the two, but you have to keep yourself focused on Kevin's needs and not your guilt over James."

"I used to take him on little adventures. He was never able to walk—always too weak. And his wheelchair… it was so specialized it cost a fortune. My parents were always warning me I'd better not damage it, because they'd reached their insurance limit for durable medical equipment and didn't have the money to buy him anything else. So one day—I was probably eight, making James six—I marched down to the hospital and told the receptionist I needed another wheelchair for my brother.

That I wanted to fix one up so I could take him places outside the house.

"She just looked at me and said, 'Young man, we're not in the business of giving away medical equipment here. You'll have to talk to your insurance provider.' Well, it about broke my heart. because I had so many big plans for James. You can imagine how crestfallen I was when I left there. But before I got back through the doors an older man signaled me over and asked what I needed the chair for. I told him about James, and how I wanted him to experience things other kids did. As it turned out, he did the wheelchair repairs for the hospital, and in his shop he had dozens of chairs. People would donate them, and he'd hang on to them until he met a worthy cause."

"You were a worthy cause?"

"Not me. James. Mr. Penrod had a small-sized chair that was perfect. He put some heavy-duty tires on it, and a couple other gadgets that would hold James upright—he never really had the musculature to sit up very long on his own. When it was done, Mr. Penrod dropped it off in his truck and from then on James didn't get left out. Wherever I went with my friends, James went, too.

"Sure, he had to be on oxygen, but Mr. Penrod had built a cylinder-holder on the chair. And, sure, James had to be strapped in a certain way—with cross-body straps. But all my friends learned how to do that, and James was never excluded unless he was tired or not feeling well. And he was such fun. Nobody ever looked at him as that little brother who always tagged along, or that kid with the disability who slowed them down. That was the best part. James was included, and everybody *wanted* to include him. They didn't do it because they had to."

A glistening smile lit Carter's eyes as tears ran down

Sloane's cheeks. "I would have liked to meet him," she said, sniffling.

"He would have loved you. At least I'd like to imagine the adult James would have. Anyway… I'm going to go check the temperature, then make final arrangements with Cruz to spot us overhead."

"Do you need me to go with you?" she asked, hoping he would say yes, but expecting him to turn her down.

"Not need so much as want." He stood, then held out a hand to her.

When she stood, he pulled her into him, and for a moment they were so close, staring into each other's eyes, it was like time was standing still. She expected what? A kiss? An embrace? But none of that happened, and she could see the change come over him. Going from desire to caution. So, she was the one who backed away. And she was the one who broke the spell that had almost come over them.

"On second thought, I think I'll run up to my room and change my…socks."

But, before she turned away, she did brush a light kiss to his lips. Not from habit this time, but from affection. Maybe they couldn't share true intimacy again, but she wasn't going to change her nature just to avoid her feelings. She loved Carter and she wasn't against showing it.

"You do know you're about to give a little boy the dream of his heart. It's all good, Carter." With that, she ran her thumb delicately over his lips, then sighed. "All good."

By the time they were ready to start their hike down Little Swallow Canyon, at least two dozen people had gathered in the lobby to see them off. People here cared. Some of these were staying at the hotel, but others lived in Forgeburn. He recognized them and was grateful for their support.

"Anything else you need?" Matt McClain asked. He was one of the well-wishers, but because he was also owner of the medical practice, he'd supplied a good many of the medical things they were going to take.

"Nerves of steel," Carter responded, his voice so quiet and concentrated, Matt could barely hear him. He held out his hands to Matt, to show how hard he was shaking.

"You're in your element doing this," Matt reassured him. "Live in the moment and have a great time."

Yes. Live in the moment. That's something he was doing a lot of these days. "I've spent the better part of the late afternoon walking up and down Dry River, trying to put together every scenario that could happen. So, I'm ready to have some fun with this. Thanks."

Matt slapped him on the back. "Well, you've got Sloane, two rangers and Kevin's parents on the ground. And Cruz has eyes in the sky, along with his dad and sister. So, you're pretty well covered. Oh, and the rangers have closed that part of the trail until you get back. They don't want people following along, or taking pictures. This is an important time for the Mallory family, and I don't want it ruined by well-intentioned people who'll simply get in the way. I hope you don't mind my interference but I knew which strings to pull to get it all set up."

"I appreciate it," Carter said, staring outside as one of the rangers brought the little trail donkey up to the door.

It had special gear rigged for Kevin—mostly to hold him on the seat and keep him upright. It was quite like the chair Mr. Penrod had rigged for James, and when Carter realized that his hands stopped shaking. This trek was nothing more than what he'd done with his brother, and back then he'd never let the thought of dire consequences get in the way."

"They're on their way," Sloane said, stepping up to Carter and slipping her hand around his waist. "Right now they're trying to calm Kevin down, because if he gets much more excited than he already is—well, his breathing…"

"Don't want to see that happen," Carter said. He turned to face her. "I know we've got a lot muddy water under our bridge—or shall I say *my* bridge—and you have no idea how much I hate that. But I want to tell you that one of my counselors at The Recovery Project has talked to me about facing my fears head-on. He said if I can't do that I'll never fully come to terms with my life, such as it is."

"I wish I knew more about what your life turned into after you left me, Carter. I do want to understand, because the man who's about to do this amazing thing for a little boy is part of the Carter I remember, and not the one who got on his motorcycle and never looked back."

"I looked back, Sloane. More than you'll ever know. All I am now is the Carter who's straddling a couple different lives. The first part of the program has taught me to see that very clearly. I'm neither one person or another. Eventually I'll know, or maybe I won't. For me, right now, it's getting by day to day. I can't set any goals other than moving along in my program, and I can't allow myself to have hopes and dreams because that puts too much pressure on me. That's my bottom line, Sloane. And it's not a very pretty one—at least, not yet. But if you truly want to get to know me, that's who I am…an aftermath, I suppose you could say. Anyway, here comes Kevin and his family, so I think it's time to get on that trail."

"Carter—one last thing before we go… The progress

is there. Maybe you can't see it yet, or it's not the kind of progress you expected. You always have been a bigger-than-life kind of guy. But I see how hard you're working, and while the changes might not be earth-shattering I can see them. I do wish I could have been the one to help you along, but that's just me needing to be involved. *All about me, not you.* You've made an excellent choice with The Recovery Project and I'm so glad it's helping you. That's all I ever wanted."

Without a thought, care or concern, Carter pulled Sloane into his arms and kissed her. It wasn't a passionate kiss that would lead to more. But it was a familiar kiss. The one he'd always given her when she'd needed reassurance. The one she'd always given him when he'd needed comforting. And this kiss lasted a good long while, until Carter pulled back and whispered, "I think we're being watched."

Sloane opened her eyes, looked around her, and sure enough they were surrounded by people. In fact the rapt attention of the crowd was so single-focused she actually expected the people to break into applause. Bu, all they got were some oohs and ahs, which were quite enough for her and, judging from the scarlet stain creeping up Carter's neck, enough for him, as well.

"So—let's do it," she said, stepping away from Carter and heading to the door, where, outside, the cutest little gray and tan donkey stood waiting.

"He's the gentlest one we have," the handler said to Sloane. "Sometimes we take him over to the children's hospital in Piperidge for the kiddies there to ride. A couple of them have problems similar to Kevin's, and Henry—my donkey—loves the attention. Don't you, boy?" he asked as he patted the donkey's rump.

"He looks perfect for Kevin." Sloane turned just in

time to see Kevin's parents wheel him out through the door. "And, judging from the look on Kevin's face I'd say he thinks so too."

"OK," Carter said, stepping up to Kevin. "We've gone over how this is going to work. I'll put you up from the left side, with some help from a ranger, while your dad fastens you in from the right. Try not to move until we get you situated—and that includes getting a helmet on you."

"Do I have to wear it?" Kevin asked. "It looks heavy."

"It has communication gear in it. You can talk to me anytime and I'll hear what you're saying. Just like I can talk to you anytime. So if you feel funny, get scared, need a drink of water, want me to hook you up to your oxygen—*anything*—tell me. Is that a deal?" he asked the boy.

"Deal," Kevin said, sticking out his hand to shake on it. "As long as you take lots of pictures."

Carter looked around, and saw that everyone there, except for Kevin himself, had either a phone or a camera ready to shoot. And as they got the boy hoisted up on Henry's back at least two dozen photos were clicked off.

He wished he'd done that with James—captured some of those memories—because in time memories faded, or took on different shades and shapes.

"Well, then…"

Carter hoisted his pack over his back. It was heavier that the pack he usually carried, and he knew that Sloane's pack was equally heavy. But it was a momentous day in a young life, and none of that mattered. Kevin was about to have the adventure of his life.

"Let's hit the trail."

He put on his own communication helmet, and they were on their way.

The trail head wasn't too far, but they took it slow and

easy, to allow Kevin to get the feel for riding Henry. And, just as Carter had expected, the jubilant crowd of onlookers followed them for the first little way.

By the time they reached the trail head most of them had dropped away—probably to get themselves ready to welcome Kevin back, which would be in about an hour.

The rangers led the donkey, followed by Kevin's parents, who flanked Henry's sides. Then, bringing up the rear, were Carter and Sloane. They were keeping themselves a fair distance back, because their desire here was to make this outing as normal as they were able to. Dragging two doctors along wasn't normal, so they stayed back, taking pictures of the vegetation, and the little lizards that would dart out of the rocks, get scared and dart right back in, and the lazy hawks circling overhead, looking for a tasty tidbit to sustain them through the rest of the day.

Even though it was heading into the evening, the sky was still so blue it was breathtaking. Every now and then they would head the rotors of Cruz's helicopter in the distance, but he never got close enough to be intrusive. For being the Los Angeles boy that he was, Carter was beginning to find some sense of purpose here in Forgeburn, and it had a lot more to do with an ideal than looking at it as his last chance. Here, he was needed. He was useful. And, he was wanted. Being in Forgeburn gave him a whole unique perspective on how to solve his problems. Or, at least, how to approach them. And this is where he wanted to be. No vacillating on the decision. He was good here. Felt good. Even felt some optimism for the first time since he'd been injured. His program had a two-month level two that he could be facing any time, then after that, a third level. Overall, he was into it for another six months, and after that—

"You're looking serious," Sloane said. "Anything you care to talk about?"

Carter glanced at her, then smiled. "Want to pose for me? That rock up ahead would be a good spot, if you don't mind climbing up on it."

"Since when have I ever backed away from a little old rock?"

She hurried to get out in front, then scaled the boulder with all the skill of a professional.

"So, how do you want me?" she called down to him. "In a victory position, hands on my hips, surveying my vast domain? Or something a little more provocative? Maybe stretching out on the rock, being interactive with it?"

"Whatever feels natural," he called out as he approached her.

"Then this…"

She simply stood there, hands clasped in front of her, a big smile on her face. She left her cap on, left her ponytail as it was, and waved to the Mallorys who, while only a hundred feet ahead, seemed as if they were in another universe, and this universe was only for Carter and her.

"Snap away."

"Already did," he said, laughing. "I have a fully documented photo file of your journey up the rock, up to and including finding your perfect position."

Sloane's response to that was to pull out her phone and snap a few photos of Carter. He photographed well. Much better than her. Always had.

"So, can I come back down now?"

"If we want to stay caught up to Kevin."

She looked at the boy, then back at Carter. "He's leaning a little too hard to the right to suit me. I think we need to take a break—get him straightened in his saddle, take his vitals, maybe make sure he's been drinking."

She scaled down the rock, then pulled a bottle of cold water from her ice pack.

"Just precautionary," she said, handing the water to Carter, who ran on ahead and stopped Kevin for a few minutes.

"He's a little bit warm," Carter said as Sloane caught up. "Lungs are good. Pulse is steady. I say we keep going once he's had some water and a protein snack I brought just to bolster him if he needed it."

To be honest, he didn't know if they did a damn thing to help. But James had always taken one along, and he'd truly believed they raised his stamina. So with Kevin it only stood to reason that if they did help it was a good thing he'd brought a few bars along. And if they didn't help maybe the placebo effect would work.

Either way, the break was necessary, because his back was starting to ache again, and Kevin did need a little down time. So, they rested for fifteen minutes, then started again, but this time with Carter walking next to Kevin, steadying himself on the donkey's rump, and pointing out various rock formations, little animals that darted away, and all the other things associated with the desert.

"I saw a common side-blotched lizard a while ago," Kevin said. "It was standing up on a rock, watching us. Didn't even move when we went by."

"Maybe he was too afraid to move," Carter said. The way *he'd* been so often this past year.

"Or maybe he just liked watching. Some people do, you know."

"You're not a watcher, are you Kevin? Because standing off to the side and watching what other people want you to see isn't much fun—especially if you have a list of things you want to do."

"I do have a list. Next thing on it's the Statue of Liberty."

Carter admired this kid, and he admired the parents who were fighting hard to give him the very essence of life that sustained him. In so many ways he was braver than Carter was. But not braver than James. His brother had written up his own wish list. Unfortunately, their parents had only allowed small wishes and dreams, while James had wanted to conquer the world.

"Would you believe I've never seen that? I've been to New York City, but only long enough to change planes and get to my next destination. I've always thought I would go back, but so far it hasn't happened."

"You should go, Doc Carter. Going to see it is better than just sitting around thinking about it. Right, Dad?" Kevin addressed his father, who was walking on the other side of the donkey.

"We do our best to give Kevin the world. It's not always easy, but we manage. And as far as the Statue of Liberty goes…maybe in the spring?"

Kevin drew in a breath that sounded a little wheezy. Nothing to get alarmed over in the world of a child with CF, but still…

Carter motioned Sloane forward with her medical supplies, pointed to his own chest and mouthed the word *wheezing.* Immediately she dropped back, sat her bag on the ground and shuffled through the supplies for an inhaler. She also pulled out her stethoscope, then stood and rejoined the party.

"Can we stop for a minute?" she called to the rangers, who responded immediately. "Kevin, I need to have a listen to your chest while Doc Carter takes your blood pressure. You OK with that?"

The child nodded—but he was anything but OK with what was happening, as could be seen by the scowl on his face when the rangers lifted him from the donkey.

After taking Kevin's blood pressure and finding it lower than he liked, Carter stepped around to talk to Kevin's parents. "I'm not going to tell you that something serous is going on, because he's only showing mild symptoms of respiratory discomfort. But I'm also not going to tell you that he's good to keep going—because I don't know yet."

"He told us he wants to fight through this," Kevin's father reiterated.

"But if he's on the verge of having problems..."

Kevin's mom took a good, hard look at her son. "It's not worth it. He's had his donkey ride, and it was the ride of his life. But I don't want it to be the ride that costs him his life."

Carter recalled the last time he'd taken James on an adventure. He really hadn't been feeling very good, but he'd wanted it so badly. He'd had friends at the park, who were going to meet him there, so Carter had taken him. After that, James had gone to bed for the rest of his life—which had been a grand total of seven days.

That was when he'd made that promise to fix his little brother, and that was also when his seven-year-old brother—with more profound wisdom than a child that age should ever have had—had taken his hand and said, *"That's OK, Carter. Sometimes things don't get fixed."*

And damn. Here he was with Kevin now. He was older and wiser, and yet still very much the nine-year-old who took all the blame on his young shoulders.

"You OK?" Sloane whispered, coming to stand next to Carter.

He shook his head. "My brother once told me some things don't get fixed."

"But this isn't your brother. It's Kevin, and he's fighting to get through this donkey ride."

"And the decision is up to me. Break his heart or take the risk."

Sloane laid her hand on the small of his back and began a circular rub. It felt good. Too good. Too distracting. Because right now the only thing he wanted was to get lost in her touch. Pretend that nothing else existed.

Except it did.

"Would you loosen his clothes, give him the inhaler, then get some oxygen in him?"

"Then the decision's made?"

Carter nodded. "For Plan A. But I do have a plan B, so keep your fingers crossed."

"It's the right thing," she said. "Kevin may not see it now, but next spring, when he goes to see the Statue of Liberty, he'll remember the doctor in Forgeburn who made the hard choice that gave him another shot at his list."

Sloane walked forward to inform the rangers, while Carter had a quick talk with Kevin's parents. Naturally they were disappointed, but they understood that a little caution exercised now was for the best.

"Well, Kevin," Carter said, stepping to the side of the big flat boulder where the rangers had lain the boy. He was drinking water, and sweating too much. "As much as I'd like to take you out of here on Henry, it's not safe. You're running a little bit of a temperature and your lungs are wheezy. You're also looking a little too tired. So, while I hate to do this, I've got to get you out of here quicker than Henry can."

Kevin didn't say a word. Instead he turned his head and didn't acknowledge Carter at all.

"But I do have another plan that may be more fun than this."

Kevin still didn't acknowledge him, and that was understandable. He was breaking the kid's heart the way his brother's heart had been broken so many times.

"Ever flown in a helicopter?"

"No," said Kevin, sniffling back tears of frustration.

"I have, and it's pretty neat. But what's even neater is the way you're going to get *into* that helicopter." He looked up and saw Cruz coming into position. "Can you see the helicopter up there?"

"Uh-huh…"

"Well, it can't land. There's no place safe around here."

This was beginning to pique Kevin's interest. "If it can't land, and I can't go up there to get on, how am I going to get to it."

"Easy. Cruz is going to drop a basket out the door. It's been well-secured inside, so it won't fall or do anything crazy. Once it reaches the ground we'll get you in it, and you'll be pulled up through mid-air, until Cruz's father and sister can pull you inside."

"You mean I'll be suspended in that basket for a little while?"

"That's exactly what I mean. And I'll go along beside you, just to make sure you don't get scared."

"Scared? Heck! I never knew I wanted to do this until now, but you *have* to let me do it, Doc Carter. It'll be like I'm flying all by myself."

Kevin's face took on a slight glow of excitement, but

his eyes told the real story. Another adventure—another way to live outside his disability.

"Well, then, let me signal Cruz to drop the basket for you and the harness for me and we'll get this party started."

He looked over at Kevin's parents, who both seemed mortified.

"It's all good," he reassured them. "Kevin gets a new adventure, and once he's in the chopper we'll simply fly him to the nearest hospital."

Not Whipple Creek. While it served as a fine first aid station, and did take care of minor problems, Kevin's condition warranted more. Especially now, before anything major occurred.

Within a minute the orange stretcher basket was floating through the sky, being watched over by the very capable Cruz family.

"Which hospital?" Cruz asked.

By now Sloane was in charge of the radio, as Carter and the rangers got Kevin into position in the basket. "Whatever you think is best."

"Then it's north, to Salt Lake City. I'll radio through to let them know what we're bringing in. Is he OK?" Cruz asked.

"Kevin? I think he's having the time of his life."

"I meant Carter. How's *he* doing?"

Sloane glanced over at him, watched the way he was strapping himself into the harness like it was an everyday thing.

"He's doing great, Cruz," she said. "Better than I've seen him do in a long, long time."

"It's Forgeburn. I tell you. There's something curative here. Good for the weary soul."

"Maybe it is," she said, and walked over to Carter. "Hospital's being taken care of and Cruz is ready to ride."

"Hear that, Kevin? We're getting ready to fly."

"Um…can I have a drink of water first? My throat seems like it's beginning to close."

Carter and Sloane exchanged worried glances, but it was Carter who came to the rescue. "It's nerves. Once you get off the ground and relax you'll feel better."

He handed Sloane the water bottle while he did a double-check on both the basket and his own harness. Then he looked up, waved to Cruz, and in the blink of an eye both Carter and Kevin were lifted off the ground. Carter's harness kept a little lower than Kevin, to prevent tangling of the lines, and in mere moments Cruz's family was pulling Kevin to safety. Then Carter.

"So, how was that?" Carter asked as he divested himself of the safety gear.

"Awesome," Kevin said, giving Carter the thumbs-up once his arms were unstrapped from his body. "Freaking awesome."

Down below, Sloane watched everything, and sighed a sigh of relief when both Kevin and Carter were safely inside the helicopter. It hovered for another couple of minutes, until everybody inside was either secure or in a position to respond should Kevin have problems.

"I heard he has PTSD," Mrs. Mallory commented as the rangers led Henry back to his owner and the rest of them cleared the area of the various bits and pieces of medical debris.

"He does."

"And he's allowed to practice?"

Sloane couldn't help but smile, She was so proud of Carter. "Not only is he allowed, he's very much needed."

"Well, what he's done for Kevin goes above and beyond, so I'm glad he's the doctor we got to see. Even something as insignificant as a donkey ride has changed Kevin's life, and that's what his father and I try to do as much as we can. You never know when…"

She choked on tears that couldn't be held back.

"It's difficult living with someone who wants so much but has time for so very little. I hope Doc Carter will stay in touch with Kevin. He'd love that."

"I'm sure he will," Sloane said. She said that because she was getting to know Carter again. And the Carter she knew now would do something like that. She was sure of it.

CHAPTER TEN

BY THE TIME Sloane woke up it was well into the morning. Something about this place made her relax in ways she'd never relaxed before. Sleeping as late as she had—that wasn't like her.

Her first thought was Carter, of course. He hadn't come back last night, but he had texted to let her know he was going to stay with the Mallory family for as long as they needed him, and that he'd be back first thing this morning.

Which meant he must already be at work.

Yesterday—watching Kevin being airlifted out and seeing Carter dangling from the helicopter in that harness, completely in control—was an awesome thing. Another reason to be proud. The crowds who'd gathered to send them off on the trail had been waving and cheering as the helicopter had flown overhead. And more people had gathered, waiting for news. and stayed gathered well into the night, until the first report on Kevin came back. It was a good one, too. Kevin's setback was only minor and he'd be out of the hospital in a couple of days. And again, the people cheered and partied even farther into the night, toasting the absent Carter off and on the whole time. She only wished he could have been there to see it—to see the impact he'd made in such a short time.

There was such camaraderie here Sloane almost couldn't see Carter working anyplace else now. To her, he'd always been big-city, big-hospital material. Someone who thrived where the odds were greater and the demands harder. But this little area was so—*him*. Every bit of it.

She wondered if he saw that. She hoped so. Because the thing she wanted most for Carter was for him to be happy. Here in Forgeburn, he *was* happy, and Sloane was beginning to see that.

Her phone rang and the identification came up with Carter's name. "You up?" he asked after her hello.

"Barely. People got together last night and, well…"

He chuckled. "Let me guess. You partied with them?"

"A little more than I should have."

"Well, if you're up for a little adventure I've got to make a call about thirty miles away from here—all of it on one of the cowboy roads. There's a hiking party out there and the trail guide's collapsed. He's alert now, but a little disoriented, and definitely not in any condition to bring the people back in. So, I thought one of us could tend to the guide while the other gets the hikers back safely. Are you up for it?"

"Do you know why he collapsed?" she asked, heading toward the shower.

"My guess is he was doing the same thing as you last night—except you don't ever drink very much, and he did. He's probably dehydrated. I told the man who contacted me to get fluids into the guy, so with any luck by the time we get there the crisis will have been averted."

"And this is in your job description?" She reached into the shower, turned it on, then waited for the water to adjust to the right temperature.

"*Everything* is in my job description. What Matt told

me when he hired me is that the diversity is the best part. As good a surgeon as he is, he loves being out here, where one minute he's chasing down a cowboy and the next he's delivering a baby."

"Well, you seem to be thriving here as well."

"Maybe not thriving so much as coming to terms with the idea that I don't belong in a hospital setting anymore. It's not easy when that's all you know. But people change, and I have to accept the fact that I'm one of them."

Carter sounded so good. It was hard to believe that this was the man who'd walked out on her just a little over three months ago.

"You're getting there, Carter," she said, wiggling out of her shorts and top while trying to balance her phone. "Look, let me grab a quick shower, then I'll meet you in the parking lot."

"Gear up," he said.

"As in motorcycle?"

"As in that's the only form of transportation I've got."

She smiled, thinking about riding behind him again. Maybe it wasn't meant to be sexual, but being in that kind of contact with him was as sexual as it got. And while it was too early in the morning to be having those kinds of thoughts, she couldn't deny them. And she never had, when they'd both awakened together in the morning with the very same thought.

"Great, just great," she said, reaching over to adjust the shower temperature to something a little colder, then bracing herself for the jolt of it. Which came. But, didn't take away those feelings.

So, she hurried through, got dressed, then by the time she opened her hotel door, Carter was standing out in the hall, waiting.

"Something wrong with your back?" she asked, noticing the way he was leaning against the wall, gingerly rubbing his lower lumbar.

"Twisted it a few days ago. Nothing serious. Not even worth getting x-rayed."

"But you're up to another hike into the desert?"

It hurt him worse than he let on. She could see it in his eyes.

"Because I could grab one of the tour guides here and we could go out."

Carter waved her off, then stepped away from the wall.

"Like I said, nothing serious."

"When was the last time you saw a doctor, Carter? Weren't you supposed to be checked every two or three months?"

"I'm fine, Sloane," he said, sounding a little bit annoyed. "Not sick, not injured. Just adjusting to more activity than I've had in a while."

She wasn't convinced, but she wasn't going to argue the point. Why bother, when Carter didn't want that kind of intrusion from her? So, instead of continuing in that direction, she grabbed up her backpack which, little by little, had filled up with medical supplies, and stepped into the hall.

"This is the new me—no mincing of words. It is what it is, Sloane. I don't mean to be harsh, but I don't want to argue about my physical condition, either."

She stopped and simply stared at him for a moment. "It wouldn't hurt you to find a nice comfortable spot in the middle. Especially if you're holding on to any thoughts of staying here."

"I *am* leaning in that direction," Carter said, as he stepped aside to let her through the elevator door first. "A lot of things are hinging on how well I do with the last two parts of my program, so for now nothing is set in stone. I'm still at the stage where I'm getting myself through day by day. But I do like it here."

As the elevator doors closed, he took his place on the opposite side from her, then continued, "It's not easy going from being someone who has his life planned out every step of the way to someone who's only able to take it a day at a time, or one challenge at a time. But I'm working at it. Not always successfully, though."

"What do you mean?"

Carter creased his face into a frown and leaned back against the wall. "I do have this idea—but it may be too far out there to consider. I've been wondering what would happen if I did come back here after I've finished the program, resume practice, maybe even buy it from Matt. Then set up a recovery program much like the one I'm going through, only with horses. Everybody around here has a horse, and there are wild horses everywhere. I know there are a couple programs already working with horses, teaching people how to handle them and even become farriers, and they're getting a lot of notice in the PTSD communities. So why not here, in Forgeburn?"

"That's a whole lot of thinking into the future," she said, reaching behind Carter to push the button. "But it sounds fantastic, provided you can recruit the right people to run it."

She was excited for him, because looking out toward others' needs, and not simply inward at his own, was unlike anything he'd done in the past year. But she had to be reserved about it, rather than plunge in and make plans with him, or try to help the way she always did. Right now, treading lightly with Carter was the way she had to go.

To what end Sloane wasn't sure. She'd come looking for peace and quiet, and yet her hopes were beginning to take over—which wasn't necessarily bad, but also wasn't good, since Carter seemed to be the one with the clearer focus now.

"I hope it works for you."

There were so many other things she wanted to say, like *Can I help you?* and *What does that mean for us?* But she didn't, because she'd been rejected by him once before and she still wasn't over it—and she certainly wasn't ready for yet another rejection.

When the elevator door opened she stepped out and walked on ahead of him without another word,

What was there to say anyway?

Carter's life was going in one direction and hers in another. In a few days she'd be back at her L.A. hospital, doing all the things she'd done before. And Carter—well, his future was wide open, and she doubted it would ever again include routine medicine. No surgical schedules, no surgical follow-ups.

What he had here—this was what he wanted, and it did suit him. It was nothing she would have seen coming. Probably nothing Carter would have seen coming either. But he was growing into a contentment she'd never seen in him before. And a different kind of focus. Something more laid-back and personal. In a way, she envied him.

"So we've got to go thirty miles to give this guy some water for his hangover?" she asked as they approached his motorcycle. "What happens if in the meantime you have a real patient who needs real skills?"

"I make the choice." He got on the bike, then held out his hand to help Sloane climb on the back. "And the people here seem to trust me to do that."

"Your skills as a doctor were never questioned, Carter. Up to and including that day you walked out, I never heard anybody question any medical decision you made."

"Then you weren't listening, Sloane. The criticisms were real—and loud. And they wouldn't let go of me no matter what I did."

"They were in your mind, Carter."

"And your mind is a terrible thing to have turn against you."

"But you're turning it around now. Remember that. You're turning it around."

Sloane fastened her helmet and wrapped her arms around his waist, and as she did so she noticed him jerk slightly to the side.

"Did I hurt you?" she asked.

"Nope. Just making an adjustment."

And that was the last thing he said before they took off. Because their helmets were not in sync for communication, they rode in silence for thirty minutes, but when they got to the site where the questionable trail guide had collapsed no one was there.

"Did we lose our patient?" Sloane asked, once they were stopped.

"Our patient *and* his party."

Carter radioed the lodge hosting the group and discovered that they'd gone on without their guide.

"Except they went in opposite directions. The group is headed to the finish of the trail and they left their guide here, sitting on a rock."

"So maybe he's gone on ahead, too?"

"According to the concierge, Kip—that's his name—was in no shape to walk anywhere. In fact they specifically told him to find another guide, that he was not to lead anyone anywhere."

Carter let out a frustrated sigh, then sat down on the rock.

He looked tired. But then yesterday had done *her* in

and she hadn't been involved in that rescue to the extent Carter had been, so maybe this was simply residual tiredness that would be fixed by a good nap.

"So, what's our next option?" she asked. "Because if you want this doctor's opinion, I think you should go back to your place and get some rest. You're not looking good, Carter."

To prove her point, Sloane took him by the wrist to check his pulse—but it seemed fine, which surprised her.

A sly grin crept over his face. "Care to examine any other parts of me? You know I'm not in the least shy about that—as long as it's you doing the exam."

That was definitely the old Carter speaking and she blushed. thinking about how many times she'd given in to his naughty persuasions.

"Yeah, right. Out here in the open, where anybody could see us."

"Look around, Sloane. We're the only ones here."

Laughing, she sat down next to him, wondering why she'd worn such a tight sleeveless T-shirt. It left nothing to the imagination, especially without a bra, and she wasn't wearing one. And what with the sweat it might be a wet T-shirt contest for all the good the stretchy fabric was doing.

Self-consciously, she crossed her hands over her chest and hunched down a little.

"No need to hide from me, Sloane," Carter said. "I've seen it all—and God knows you know how much I've always liked that aspect of our relationship."

"Except our relationship is over, Carter."

"But the memories linger…" He reached over and traced the line of her collarbone with his index finger. "And they're good ones."

She thought about slapping his hand away, but too

much of her wanted this. Wanted his touch and so much more. Because they were good at this. Maybe too good. So many of the other aspects of their years together seemed to fade away, but not those details.

"Were we ever right for each other?" she asked. "I know we had a lot of years, but you were gone for so many of them I'm wondering if we ever got past the physical attraction."

Carter pulled his hand away. "Seriously? You think in all that time that's all we had?"

"I'm at a place right now where I question everything. The way we are now—it's hard to put us together the way we were back then. We did things together all the time, and that was good. But I wonder who were we that you didn't feel inclined to tell me something so important as that you needed space and encouragement, not someone to jump in and take over and try to fix you. So, yes, I do question things now."

Sloane noticed his hands shaking and wondered if he was on the verge of a PTSD incident. Shaking hands was always a giveaway—one that told her to tread very carefully. Was she pushing him into this?

"I don't have an answer for you because I always thought we were good."

"So did I—but were we really good enough? We were almost married by the time you left. My wedding dress is still hanging in the closet."

Carter wiped the sweat off his face, then studied his shaking hands for a moment before he spoke.

"By that time we weren't good. At least I wasn't. And it killed me watching you trying to help me all the time, especially when I knew nothing was working. I never meant to hurt you, Sloane. But, honestly, at the point when I left the only person I could think about was me.

I hated seeing you cry, which was happening more and more, and I didn't want to be responsible for that. I didn't want to be responsible for me, either."

He wiped his brow again, then crammed his shaking hands into his pockets.

"Is something going on I should know about?" she asked, her level of concern rising at seeing so many physical symptoms she remembered. Shaking hands. Sweating. Shortness of breath. A relentless restlessness that kept elevating. And his restlessness was definitely elevating. In fact he was so antsy he hopped off the rock and started to pace.

"No, I'm fine."

But he wasn't. And here they were, right back where they'd used to be. He was leaving her out. Something was obviously wrong, and she wasn't being included in it.

"Well, I say we call the rangers and let them worry about our errant tour guide and his hikers, then we can head back to the hotel."

He stopped for a moment to look at her, but it was a strange look. One that was almost looking right through her.

"Sloane, I—" He stopped. Gasped for breath. Then bit down hard on his lower lip. "I need help…" he gasped.

Then he collapsed into her arms.

Her first reaction was to lower him to the ground. Then feel for a pulse in his neck—it was there, but thready.

"Carter, can you hear me?" She had no idea what this was. Certainly not PTSD. "Carter…?"

Grabbing his medical bag, she pulled out his stethoscope and listened to his chest. It was clear. When she checked his blood pressure it was strong enough. But his ankles were slightly swollen. As were his hands. And his breathing was…labored.

She thought back to his stitch of pain earlier, when she'd climbed on to the motorcycle. And his tiredness. And all the other little things: his shaking hands; his sudden irritability. She thought hard for a moment, running down the list of things she'd observed, things she'd been worried about then, suddenly, it hit her, as did a mammoth bout of nausea.

"Carter!" she said, picking up her phone and hoping she had enough bars out here to ring Cruz.

Because Carter was dying.

She believed his remaining kidney had failed or was in the process of it and, while she wasn't a specialist, she knew that if she was correct, he needed dialysis as fast as possible or the toxins that weren't being filtered due to kidney failure would kill him.

"Hang in there with me, Carter. I think you've got a kidney problem going on." Naturally, she didn't expect him to respond. But she hoped he would.

"Hear you've got a semi-sober trail guide out there," Cruz said after he answered his phone.

"I have a patient in renal failure. I need to get him to the hospital, so can you track me and come get us?"

"I'll be right out to you," he assured her. Then, "Since you went out with Carter—is it him?"

"It is," she said, fighting back the panic and the fear rising in her. "And it's bad. He's unconscious."

"Ten minutes tops."

Which would turn into the ten longest minutes of Sloane's life.

"Look Carter," she said, sitting in the middle of the dry, dusty dirt road with Carter's head in her lap. "I understand why you weren't taking your health seriously. You were fighting such a huge battle and your life was getting better. But to ignore this? Sure, maybe you didn't want another obstacle in your way, but this is your life we're dealing with."

She lifted his limp hand to her lips and kissed it.

"How could you do this to yourself, to me. To us?"

Any other time the tears would have been flowing, but she was in full doctor mode and when she was a doctor, she didn't cry. Never. But she was so close because she was scared. This was the man she'd loved more than life for six years and he was dying in her arms.

"It's not going to happen. I won't allow it." she said, trying to move herself into a position where her body shaded his.

Allow it? Right. As if she had any control over his condition.

"We've come too far, for too long, to end it here, this way, Carter. Whether you want to hear this or not, I've loved you so much and for so long, and while I got frustrated with you so many times this past year. But that didn't mean I didn't love you, because I did. And I still do. Nothing about that has changed. And I'm pretty sure you love me."

Sloane wiped his sweaty brow with the bottom of her shirt.

"I don't know if we can fix things. But I want to try again. I deserve it. *We* deserve it."

She glanced up to see if Cruz was on his way, but the sky was empty.

"And if that means I move to Forgeburn and turn myself into a GP, that's what I'll do. It's called being in love, and somewhere along the way I think you forgot how to do that. But I want it back, Carter. Do you hear me? I want all of it back."

Sloane assessed his vitals again and found there was essentially no change.

"I may not have been forceful enough when we were together before, or maybe I was too forceful—I don't know. But it was because I loved you so much."

Even though the tears were threatening harder now, she still wasn't going to cry. Carter needed her to be a doctor, needed her to save his life. And the way she was going to do that—he might not approve but, at least, he'd be alive to argue with her about it.

"So here's the plan. Carter. Cruz is going to fly you to the hospital to get you fixed. After that, you and I are going to quit all this avoiding the real situation, and deal with it. Like, how you still love me. She brushed back the damp hair from her face.

"Because I love you, and that's the only way I know how to take care of you. For me, Carter, it's all or nothing. And I want it all."

The distant sound of a motorcycle startled her out of her moment, and she looked up to see Matt coming to a stop. He grabbed an armload of supplies from his storage and came running to her.

"Cruz called me. He's delayed a little longer than he should be, and since I was already in the vicinity…"

"IV," Sloane said, snapping back into doctor mode.

She had a patient to take care of here. The most important patient of her life.

Carter opened his eyes, but nothing came into focus except a white ceiling. He stared up at it for a moment. Then he blinked, wondering if it would go away. But it didn't, which meant it was real. He fixed on the ceiling for a full minute before he finally turned his head and saw the IV line in his arm—a sight with which he was well-acquainted—and the stand-by ventilator next to the bed. There were other monitors too—for blood pressure, heart-rate.

As he twisted a bit, to see what else he was hooked up to, a sharp pain stabbed him in the side. Slowly he twisted left and saw the patient in the bed next to him. He couldn't bring him into focus, though.

"Where are we?" he asked, wondering if his roomie was even awake.

His roomie sat up. That much he could see.

"Carter?"

"Sloane?" Something was off here, and he couldn't even begin to make sense of it. "What's going on?"

"You collapsed. It seems your kidney shut down and you've been suffering from uremia for a while. Uremia, by the way, has symptoms you should have noticed. You know, your back cramps, lack of appetite, excessive tiredness."

"Are you here to nag at me for not diagnosing myself?" Carter asked, so glad to hear her voice that if he could have hopped across to her bed he would have.

"It's a tough job, but…"

"Somebody's got to do it? I know. So what did they do? Dialyze me."

"Too late for that. Your kidney was—let's just say *done*."

They'd removed his kidney? No way in hell. "Seriously, what did they do to me?"

"They couldn't save it, Carter. Your binges for the past year…they took a toll. I'm sorry it happened this way, but there was nothing they could do."

He was so tired. Too much pain. And he simply couldn't take it in. No kidney meant dialysis for the rest of his life. That would take him out of The Recovery Project. Force him to move somewhere close to a dialysis center. End his medical career. End everything he'd fought so hard to get back.

"So, I'll add that to my list, right? No spleen, no kidneys, and I'll never know when my PTSD will trigger. I mean, what's the point? What's the damn point to any of this?"

"You mean what's the point of being so loved by a small community that they're raising funds to give you a proper home there? People *love* you, Carter. They depend on you. You are such a good person—such a good doctor.

"Yeah, well, tell them to skip the home and buy me a dialysis machine. Because that's the way the rest of my life is going to be written."

"Only if you want it to be," she said.

"And what's my alternative?"

"Keep the kidney they transplanted into you healthy. You know…live the better life, do the better thing."

"I—I had a *transplant*?" He looked over at her, his vision slowly returning. But not enough to really see her yet. "How? I wasn't even on the list."

"A perfect match donor came forward."

"And just *gave* me a kidney?" Now he was totally confused. People didn't just give away kidneys. Sure, the body only needed one healthy kidney, but most people opted to hang on to the other one just to be on the safe side.

"Something like that."

"Tell me how it happened. Especially since I didn't consent to it."

"You didn't have to. Remember all those years ago when you joined the Army, and you gave me your power of attorney to make decisions if you couldn't make them yourself? I still have your power of attorney, Carter. You never had it revoked after we split up, and I made the medical decision. There was a kidney available, and because of your condition you went to the top of the list. So—"

"So someone's tragedy saved my life?"

The doctors had talked to him about the possibility of a transplant at some time in the future, if the one kidney he had went bad, and being a surgeon himself there was nothing he didn't know about the whole process from start to end. But he'd never really thought in terms of having a transplant, even though he'd known his existing kidney was fragile. Now that it was done, he wasn't sure what to think.

"Do we know anything about the donor?" he asked, the way any doctor would ask. Hiding behind his medical credentials right now seemed the safest place to be. It was the only place he truly understood.

"We do. It's a woman. About your age. Well-educated. A doctor, in fact."

Carter swallowed hard. "And the match? How close was it?"

"It was a perfect match in all three categories. Blood type was perfect—both you and your donor were type B. I know that's a little bit rare, but you got lucky. The cross-match was perfect as well. And the HLA testing came out just fine. As far as a match goes, you couldn't have done any better."

"When?" he asked. "When did this all happen?

"Late yesterday—a few hours after they got you to the hospital. You were unconscious, because your kidney had bled quite a bit, so the surgery took a while longer than it normally would have. But they put you in intensive care overnight, then brought you up here to this room a few hours ago. Your vitals are stable, your incision is good—everything either of us would want to see in our surgical patients."

"And how long have *you* been here?"

"I flew in with you and haven't left."

"You didn't have to stay."

"Actually, I did. The doctors here wouldn't let me go. Although I will say it was difficult, persuading them to put a man and a woman in the same room. But after I explained how we'd lived together for so many years, and seeing that it was my kidney you were getting..."

"Stop! Did you say *your* kidney?"

"My kidney. Back in Germany, when they removed your first one and told me your second kidney could be living on borrowed time, I had myself tested as a donor just in case it ever came to that."

"And you never told me?"

"I intended to at some point, but the relationship turned so bad it never seemed like the right time. Then, when you left me—well, let's just say that I wasn't giving it a lot of thought because there were other more important things on my mind."

"*Why*, Sloane? Why would you do something like that? Especially with the way I treated you?"

"Love is bigger than any illness, Carter. You don't just stop loving someone because they're ill. Sometimes I thought I didn't love you, but it never really sank in because I knew all along that nothing about the way I felt for you was different. I loved you that very first day and I never stopped. We did get misdirected. But that's fixable. The thing is, I think we both fell into that trap of thinking that hiding the truth from each other was a good way to protect them. But it's not that way. Hiding the truth only hurts more when it's revealed. And eventually most truths *are* revealed.

"I should have told you that I would be the one stepping forward should you ever need a transplant, but I didn't because I was afraid that if you knew that it would change who we were. And you should have told me how your brother has affected your life in so many ways. It would have made a difference in the way I perceived you."

"And you gave me a kidney?"

"You always were difficult to shop for...and you do have a birthday coming up in a few days."

"Don't joke about this, Sloane. You gave up a *kidney*. Do you know what that means?"

"In terms of recovery time—a few weeks."

"In terms of your life, Sloane. *In terms of your life*."

"It means she loves you more than she loves herself, you idiot," Matt McClain said as he entered the room. "I tried talking her out of it, but the lady is stubborn. She wouldn't listen to me. Wouldn't listen to her dad, either."

"He's here, too?" Carter asked.

"At the hotel right now. But he'll be here in a little while." Matt pulled a chair in between the two hospital beds and sat down. "I can only stay a couple minutes, because Cruz needs to get back. But just listen to this—*both of you*. Sloane, you're an idiot for hanging on to this man. He's put you through hell and you don't deserve that. And, Carter, you're just an idiot, period. Walking away from the best thing you'll ever have in your life... If there's a word stronger than idiot, that's what you are. I love you both, and you know that. But you've got to do better. Because if Carter is going to stay here and continue his practice—and God only knows why the people of Forgeburn want that, but they do—that means Sloane's going to stay here, too, so you're going to have to face up to your problems, then deal with them. So, Sloane, tell the man what you want to say. And, Carter, listen to her. That's all I've got to say."

With that, he stood up, scooted the chair back, and headed for the door.

"Ellie's made up the guestroom for when you get out of here. *One guestroom.* We expect you'll be staying with us for a while, until you're stronger. And, Carter, you still owe me that motorcycle ride into the canyons."

Matt smiled as he left the room.

"It's going to work out," he told Harlan Manning as they passed in the hall. "They've got an awful lot of obstacles right now, but when they come to their senses and figure out they're still together they'll be fine. In the meantime, I think they need some time alone. Care to follow me home? Ellie's fixing enchiladas and Spanish rice tonight."

"Sounds good to me," Harlan said. "But are you sure about Sloane and Carter?"

"I told them they were both idiots. What more is there to say?"

"Now what?" Sloane asked. "We've been avoiding each other for so long I don't even know where to begin."

"Is this where we're supposed to embrace and tell each other everything's going to be all right? Because it won't be, Sloane. I may have a new lease on my physical life, but that has nothing to do with—with the reason I left you in the first place."

"Which is?" she asked, desperately wishing they could embrace.

"I couldn't hurt you anymore. I saw it happen over and over. Saw you brace yourself to take it on the chin, then get back up and take it again. And I saw you crying, Sloane. That was the worst of it. I made you cry so many times."

"It wasn't easy, Carter. Never knowing when something would trigger you. Never knowing when I'd have the real you or have to deal with your PTSD. But I coped. And I tried to help."

"I know that. I could always see it, even when I was in panic or rage mode. I always saw what it was doing to you, but I couldn't control it. It was like someone else was taking me over. Someone I couldn't control. And it scared me. Still does. Which is why I left. Not because I didn't love you. But because I loved you too much. More than my own life. Sloane, I always have. Always will."

"But you're getting through it, Carter. I called your counselor and told her what had happened, and she told me how hard you're working. They're very optimistic for you, and they'll hold your spot open in the next phase of the program until you're physically able to participate in it."

"Thank you," he said. "Thank you for everything you've done, even when I wasn't being very appreciative."

"That's what you do for your other half, Carter, and you've been my other half since the day we met. And even when you left me."

"I saw how I couldn't live up to the man I used to be, and I knew you wanted him back. After a while I figured you were staying out of pity, and that was the worst—thinking you had going from loving me to pitying me. You needed better than anything I could give you or would ever be able to give you."

"You didn't think your love was enough?" Sloane asked.

"For you, Sloane, I didn't think anything about me was enough."

"I've never stopped loving you, Carter. You've been difficult, but my love has been unconditional through everything. Because when you weren't difficult you were the Carter I fell in love with. I could always see him, even when you couldn't. And I always believed in him. So, how did we get here, Carter? Loving someone shouldn't be done in fear. But that's all we've had for the last year. I remember the night before you shipped out to Afghanistan, when we talked for hours, made promises. The promise I remember the most was that no matter what happened while you were gone it wouldn't tear us apart. That you'd come home to me and I'd wait for you. But that didn't happen. You never came home to me."

"It's hard losing yourself, Sloane. But what's harder is losing yourself and then getting occasional glimpses of who you are only to have them ripped away from you."

"And you couldn't tell me this?"

"I couldn't tell you anything, because to have done so would have meant it was true, and I didn't want it to be true. I wanted to be *me*, Sloane. I wanted to come back home to the life we had. But I didn't get any of that, and all I had left was a pretty good way to block it out of my mind or deny it when I couldn't. To admit it made it real, and I just couldn't face anything else. Not by myself. And yes, I wanted to talk to you about so many things, including the deterioration in my physical health—my backaches, my lethargy—but that would have dragged you in to it more than you deserved. So, I lied about it to you, and even to myself. And with all that, there was still my PTSD to consider." He shrugged. "I'm overwhelmed right now, Sloane. There's so much to deal with and I'm afraid of getting lost or taking the wrong direction again."

Finally the tears came, but Sloane didn't say anything for a few moments as she took in everything he was telling her. He was scared, she was scared. Yet instead of letting that fear bring them closer together, they'd let it separate them. But maybe they had needed to get here this way, to understand better how love could last through battles.

And love did last. Hers had.

"We're stronger together than we are apart, Carter. That was never addressed in any of the therapy you received when we were still togetehr. In fact, I think it was overlooked in pretty much everything I read. But the fact is you and I may fall into someone's statistical category for the bad things that happen when someone you love suffers from PTSD, but there is no statistical category for the good things. And *we* are the good things. What we were, what we had and still have..."

Sloane shut off her IV, removed the catheter from her vein, then slipped out of her bed and into bed next to Carter. It was a tight fit, but a good fit, especially when he pulled her into his arms and held her."

"I don't want to hurt you," she whispered.

Carter nodded toward one of his IV bags. "I'm covered. But you're not, Sloane. Not in the whole scheme of things."

"Do you love me?" she asked him.

"Of course I do. I've never stopped."

"Do you trust me?"

"I always have."

"Will you take care of me?"

"I've always tried. And I'll never stop trying."

"Then I'm covered." She leaned up and brushed a light kiss on his lips. "Besides, I made a pretty hefty investment in you yesterday. I think I should stick around and see how that investment pays off."

"Why did you do it?" he asked.

"Would you have done the same for me?"

"I would give my life for you, Sloane. From that first day we met nothing about that has changed."

"And I would do the same. But luckily all you needed was a kidney. As they say, easy-peasy."

And it had been. The instant Sloane had known Carter would lose his only kidney she'd stepped up. No hesitation, no fear. All she'd known was that the man she loved needed something she could give him, so how could she not?

"I'm beginning to remember why I fell so hard for you, so fast," he said, holding on to her as tight as he could, considering his condition.

"Because I'm a catch. I may not always get it right, but when I do it turns out brilliantly."

"As in…?"

"Us. You and me. Carter Holmes and Sloane Manning—meant to be."

"Even in Forgeburn?"

"Even in Forgeburn!"

EPILOGUE

"I'M GOING TO miss this place," Sloane said, settling into Carter's arms, on the porch swing. "It's so peaceful here. And all those baby bears…"

"Sounds like someone's got a mommy craving."

"Well, I'm not getting any younger…"

Carter chuckled. "We could always bump up the plan. You know how I feel about starting a family."

"But we've broken ground on the hospital already, and you've got all your licenses in line to start your new PTSD program. All that besides our medical practice. Are you going to be OK, Sloane, as a GP? Because the world's losing one of its great heart surgeons."

"I've been tucked up here in the mountains off and on for the past six months with you and nobody's even noticed I was gone."

She'd gone with Carter to the second part of his recovery program and taken advantage of the support offered for families and other loved ones. Occasionally, she'd gone back to Los Angeles, or Forgeburn, to work on their future together—the one where they would build a small, but much needed hospital in Forgeburn. But even a day or two away from him had been tough on her.

But, she'd come to Tennessee to stay on through the third part of his program because what she realized was the help was always there if she wanted it. And she wanted it and needed it almost as much as Carter did. Because she had finally come to understand that she needed it if she and Carter were to make a go of their relationship.

They had to be on the same side, fighting the same battle together, and most of all always knowing what was going on with the other one. There wasn't an easy fix, but with the support of The Recovery Project and other groups like it she was positive she and Carter would make it. There was too much love between them to let their relationship fail.

"Sounds like we're going to be busy."

"Which is why I'd like to buy a cabin up here somewhere, for when we get overwhelmed. Which, by the way, will be in about seven months."

"Seriously?" Carter asked, pulling her T-shirt up to look at her belly.

"Nothing showing. Just took the test the morning."

"So we're expanding in all directions!"

"That seems to be the case. So, are you happy that I bumped up our plan?"

It hadn't been intentional, but it was meant to be. A family of three, or more. It was a promising future, and an exciting one.

Carter grinned and pulled her even tighter. The rusting chain on the porch swing gave a little, with some creaks and groans, but like Carter and Sloane it wasn't about to give up.

"I think I may have had something to do with bumping up the plan."

"Could be..." she said.

She'd come to love the lazy evenings here. They had their own cabin, and while it wasn't secluded from the rest of the program's facilities it was far enough away that it felt like they were in a world all their own.

Tonight was especially beautiful, with the pink glow over the mountains, the darker blues above it, the lazy call of a hawk out on its evening routine.

For a little while it had been a perfect world for the two of them, and she was going to miss it. But Carter was through his program now, and it was time to get back to real life—which would be hectic and unpredictable and just as beautiful as life here had been.

Sloane laid Carter's hand on her belly. "If it's a girl I think we should name her after your first cub—Buttercup. And if it's a boy we'll name him after your second cub—Napoleon," she said with a grin.

She was so glad Carter was seeing more days of calmness and less of turmoil. And while the next part of their life might be a challenge for him, he wasn't alone in his struggles. He had Matt and Ellie, and Cruz—everybody in Forgeburn. And most of all he had her, and their baby-on-the-way.

PTSD might try to take over, but it wasn't going to win because Carter was one of the lucky ones. He was loved. So loved.

"Care to dance?" Sloane asked him.

And they did. On the pine needles. On the top of the mountain. In the glow of the setting sun.

* * * * *